No Other Pearl

- Stories -

R. Garcia Vazquez

R. Garcia Vazquez

No Other Pearl

(in the dark folds of life)

SPINNING WORLD PRESS

Spinning World Press

Copyright © 2018 by R. Garcia Vazquez

Published in the United States by Spinning World Press
Toms River, N.J.

Library of Congress Control Number: 2017919314
No Other Pearl / R. Garcia Vazquez

Softcover ISBN: 978-0-692-03500-9
Hardcover ISBN: 978-0-9991522-4-9
eBook ASIN: B079C6RHQM

Printed in the United States of America.
10 9 8 7 6 5 4 3 2 1

For

Ramon, Miguel, and Anais

*To love or have loved, that is enough, ask
nothing further. There is no other pearl to be
found in the dark folds of life.*

— Victor Hugo

Contents

The God of Beautiful Sorrows

Summer 2014

IN THE BROAD SPRAY of morning sunlight, when oak and poplar shadows stretch like giants across the front lawns of our quiet street, she comes to me wet and wild, doing her loose-hipped, end-of-six-mile-run swagger, arms akimbo, and fast round breaths issuing from her puckered mouth.

"Francis," she says in a voice flecked with humor and desire.

"I'm listening," I say, as I sweep a strand of her damp brown hair over her ear.

"Today is the most beautiful day of all," she proclaims and savors the morning air with her tongue, its taste inducing a tangled pleasure of mind, heart, and spirit. But her delight is qualified somehow, and her words echo like a sweet, futile prayer that begs for certainty and permanence.

"Taste it, Francis."

"Let me see how it tastes," I say, and drink of her tangy, responsive mouth. "But didn't you say *yesterday* was the most beautiful day ever?"

"Your point being?" she replies, drawing back.

"You are the eternal optimist. That's my point."

And yet, she's not, and I'm not sure why I go along with it. She's a false optimist, compelled to bend reality just enough to make things seem perfect. I should have discerned the vulnerability flitting behind her daring gaze and smile the moment she, Sophie Kaminski, stepped into my *Twentieth Century American Literature* class.

Maybe I did. I probably did. Yes, I did.

But the way she looked at me, and the way she smiled, had promised mornings like this. Something, or someone, sent her to me. Fate? Luck? God?

At what cost?

In all her resplendent beauty and intelligence—and despite my unceasing assurances—my urban flower labors under the weight of a question she dare not ask: *Francis, do you love Kate more than me?*

Even so, I remain in awe of her. Of her city girl smarts and ambition. Of how exuberant a lover she is. Of how tantalizingly put together. She bends and stretches with unaffected grace, her mind occupied with secret thoughts.

It was on a sunlit morning like this back in 1989, that Adam called the house. Did he first try reaching me at the university? I've wondered about that far too many times. Kate picked up the phone. "Alison is dead," Adam said, and then he broke.

When Sophie is finished stretching, she gazes at me as if I am a stranger. *But, my love, don't you know how I adore you?*

Is it too much? How many times have I said those words? I will not say them today. I will not let my love become redundant, my words meaningless.

Her expression is magically transformed, her voice energized. "Must hurry, lift weights, eat, shower, go to work, do great things, etcetera."

Winter 1987

AFTER TOO MANY drinks, I broke the news Kate was pregnant with our third child. (Kate couldn't bring herself to do it.) And just as I had envisioned, Adam glanced helplessly at Alison before standing up to congratulate us. Alison rose from her chair, forcing one last sip of her whiskey sour, and negotiating her conflicting emotions with wrenching care. Even now I can feel her cool fingers on my cheek, her cold wet lips brushing the corner of my mouth.

"How beautiful, congratulations, you two," she said with a sacrificial smile, and fluttered away like a bruised butterfly. Kate followed her to the kitchen, treading carefully.

Winter 1990

THE ODOR OF ROAST LAMB, golden-brown potatoes and red peppers should have heralded a healing feast for lovers.

I set my briefcase down, positioned myself behind Kate, and wrapped my arms around her. I whispered love in her ear. She turned from the stove and fixed me with a puzzling look.

"Adam's coming to dinner," she said, and hesitated, as though wanting to say more, but she did not. I withdrew, like one poked in the groin with a stick, muttering big-hearted words to set her at ease.

After her best friend died, it was as if a wall had risen between us. I contemplated that peculiar tendency of the wounded to hurt those they love most, and I vowed I would be patient. I would wait for my Kate, however long it took.

Adam had stayed away from our home for months. He said little and seemed content to sprawl on the living room floor with Lisa, Irene, and Virginia. I watched them play and felt a melancholic intoxication, enhanced, no doubt, by too much wine.

I watched Adam on all fours wagging his tail and grunting. My girls squealed in delight as they clutched at him and climbed over his back as though he were a well-trained bear. Adam would have made a wonderful father. Maybe someday he would become one.

When he finished his game with the girls, I stood up to embrace him, and to profess my unconditional fidelity to the cause of his happiness. My mind summoned words directly from my heart, but before I could release them, Adam turned his head and looked right past me.

I was invisible, I realized with a shock. With a distressed look, he silently thanked Kate and choked back tears. She responded with a mournful smile, pressing her hand over her mouth. Their two faces appeared cracked, as though struck by the same rod.

I pretended—not that it mattered to anyone—that my intent had been to stretch my legs and back. I sat back down and became engrossed with the strangeness of hands, with their unique way of conveying one's state—Kate's grief-holding hands, for instance, my daughters' joy-clutching hands, and my own stiff, useless hands.

Summer 2014

SOPHIE LIKES HER NEW JOB. She is the comptroller for a small software development company. "There is absolutely no difference between *comptroller* and *controller*," she asserts, "but Carson and I talked about it and decided I was the company comptroller, not controller, *comp* being user-friendly and in sync with *compatibility*, *compassion* and *computers*, whereas *cont*, as in *contrary*, *contentious* and *controlling* conjures up someone with a personality disorder."

She giggled in a way I'd never heard or seen. Who taught you to giggle like that, I wondered? Was it Carson and his cleft-lip-concealing mustache that taught you?

"Nobody likes a control freak," she says with sudden gravity, like a drunk attempting to reclaim her dignity. I stare at her, mystified.

She further tells me that she and Carson Stackey, her boss, are the *old farts* in the company, and can you believe it?

Hmm. Sophie is thirty-one. I scratch my hip contemplatively.

"Carson says he is thirty-seven going on forty-seven," she adds with a strange laugh.

"And I'm fifty-eight going on sixty-eight," I joke, and she stops laughing. "You did tell me Carson was married, right? What's his wife's name?"

"Mel," Sophie replies, "Mel, as in Melancholy."

Fall 2014

THE AROMA OF VEAL, mushroom, peppers and onion tenderizing in wine sauce triggers within me a profound sense of anticipation. I half believe Sophie will tell me Adam, whom she's never met, and whom I haven't seen in over twenty years, is coming to dinner. I secretly chide myself, but clearly, something is afoot. Over coffee and chocolate cake, my suspicion is confirmed.

"Francis? I need to tell you something."

"Is that so?" I say hoping for a smile, but levity, at the moment, is as remote as Pluto.

"I'm pregnant."

"Ho!" I cry in self-defense. I feel as if she's dropped a bowling bowl on my head.

But how can this be? Had I not told her from the start my baby-making days were over? Had I not told her this more than once before tying the knot, just to make sure we were on the same page? Did she not understand what getting *snipped* meant?

As the shockwaves recede, I search her eyes and find anxiety nestled there. Against a rising tide of mistrust, I tell Sophie I love her and kiss her abruptly and too hard. Our teeth collide. I kneel on the floor, wrapping my arms around her waist and pressing my ear to her womb. It has been known to happen, I suppose. Some might call it a *miraculous conception*.

"Oh, wow, wow, wow," I groan.

She strokes my thinning hair and absently begins to gather it in strands that she pulls too hard. A knot tightens in my upper back just below my left shoulder blade, and my right knee begins to quiver faintly against the hardwood floor.

I almost jokingly implicate her boss, but remain mute at the sobering vision of Carson Stackey smashing winners over a volleyball net during the past company picnic, his linebacker chest heaving mightily beneath damp white cotton. And behind him, in a remote corner of the court, Mel—a pretty woman in her own right, if somewhat out of shape and sullen—awaiting her opportunity to shank the ball out of play.

I say to Sophie's belly, "Let's leave the dishes. Let's go upstairs to celebrate."

But she is utterly consumed by thought.

"Tell me, sweetheart," I say, nudging my head up into her breasts. "Tell me what you're thinking."

I look up, startling her, my unpersuasive cheerfulness coaxing from her mouth a tortured smile.

Spring 1990

ADAM APPEARED at our door late one evening with a smile on his face and a newspaper under his arm. He spread the paper on the dining room table and pointed to what looked like a travel agency ad depicting a swimming pool, palm trees and a handsome couple reclining side by side on chaise lounges.

The contact for the ad read, *Adam Tyne - Eligible Bachelor.*

He could barely contain his enthusiasm as he described his plan. We did not question his judgment, nor the merit of his enterprise. After all that he had been through, how could we not encourage him and be supportive?

Adam had found a reason to hope again, and remarkably, though he was unaware of this, his unorthodox scheme produced an immediate and unexpected effect on Kate and me. It was as if his reentry into the risky realm of love had set us free.

After he left, we raced upstairs to our bedroom and fell upon one another with unbridled passion. I made no effort to understand what was happening. Reason was superfluous. We breached the limits of erotic agony and pleasure, spending ourselves as though the fate of the universe hinged on our ability to consume one another, to eradicate all trace, every last molecule, of who we were as individuals.

But something felt wrong. As I lay exhausted in the early morning hours, my heart wavering between gratitude and fear, I wondered what was to become of us, all of us.

On an impulse, I stopped at the mall that Saturday morning on my way to get a haircut. Adam did not see me. He stood by a folding table near the entrance to a ladies' boutique surrounded by numerous women. He looked like a celebrity in his blazer and turtleneck as he distributed fliers and applications. Some of the women wore alert, greedy expressions, like those of experienced bargain hunters. A reporter and a photographer from the local newspaper occupied him for a short while. Adam was poised and charming. He smiled and joked with the women and graciously endured their clumsy kisses and embraces.

Sitting in my car in the parking lot, I grew suddenly apprehensive, as if I'd forgotten to complete some important task, or as though someone had failed to inform me about an essential matter.

Winter 2015

SOPHIE IS TALKING gibberish as I try to lift myself up from the floor, but my knees have locked like rusted gears. It is the worst time for this. She looms over me, immense-bellied, her engorged breasts distant mountains. Her sandal-clad feet are swollen and splitting.

Don't worry, darling, I garble as if submerged in water.

She cannot hear me. Can she see me? As I lean forward to kiss her feet, she withdraws slowly, like a land mass shifting. I sniff the floor where her feet were, which smells of strawberries and cream tinged with vinegar.

I grow woozy, tumble sideways, and curl up on the floor in the fetal position. I try to stretch, twist and rock to generate enough momentum to flip myself back up onto my feet, but I fail repeatedly. My cheek, arm and leg have adhered to the floor. I pant like a hound. My hanging tongue is as swollen and black as an eggplant.

Sophie returns, rumbling forth like a tempest, and bearing an uncanny resemblance to the Venus of Willendorf. Her expanding life-bearing flesh is desecrated by an ever-shrinking golden bikini. She casts a hard glance my way, but barely registers my presence. Then she veers suddenly, her great flanks bounding as she lumbers out the front door. I thrash and whimper, and finally the floor loosens its hold on me.

I stumble to the front door and run across the lawn to the newspaper lying on the freshly mowed grass. Then, out of the air itself, Sophie reappears, the bikini nowhere in sight. She is completely naked now, a preposterous mass of pale bulging flesh pitching toward me like a tsunami. Her terrible expanding face reveals the countenance of a distressed angel.

I fall to my knees and raise my trembling beggar hands, and Sophie passes through me like fog through morning air.

Spring 1990

HAVE YOU MET CLAUDIA? Or seen the 8½ by 11-inch glossy of her sandwiched between two bare-chested men in leotards, three pale faces lifted in various degrees of ardent vacuity?

Despite her appeal to the lesser instincts, Claudia proved surprisingly literate, tricking Adam and me into spending more time than was prudent evaluating her application and creative insights, a choice which, consequently, prompted Kate to retire for the night earlier than she had planned. Adam stood up, attempting to remedy the matter, but Kate shushed him with a feeble smile, bringing her index finger to her lips as she climbed the stairs.

Adam stuffed the applications in his briefcase. I walked out with him into the cool night air. We stopped outside his front door. I informed him Kate would probably not be up to screening any more applications, but I could come over another evening or two to help him out, if he wanted.

"I don't want to keep you away from Kate," he said, and shook his head enigmatically.

What did he mean, keep me away from my wife? How so?

I reacted oddly to his remark, I admit. My reaction was irrational and stupid.

It's nothing, I told myself. *Do not turn it into something.*

"Not at all, Adam. We're here for you, remember that."

He nodded dismally, and we went back into our homes, reluctant duelists tramping in the meadows of loss.

Winter 2015

SOPHIE WANTS TO BE Wonder Woman. She wants to work until she births. "Until I *birth*, not *burst*," she jokes, in an attempt to smooth away the lines of tension that appear on my face whenever she mentions work.

I walk away intending to read a few more of my students' papers. Sophie is vexed by my silence and withdrawal, but I am back after sleepwalking through one paper.

"What are you making?" I ask congenially.

It's obvious she's making lasagna, but I kiss her ear and continue my foolishness. "Tell me, what's that you're making?"

"Francis?"

"Yes, hon?"

"We should talk."

I ignore the suggestion and pull away. "Call me when dinner's ready," I say, and head back to my desk. I pick up the next paper off the pile and read the title, "Why I Dumped My Boyfriend of Three Years," by Alicia Paley. First line: "Because I stopped hating him, but I guess I should explain..."

I can't do this right now. With a slow sweep of my arm, I shove everything on my desk to the side and lay my head down on my hands.

Spring 1990

THE PHOTOGRAPH grabbed me by the throat. I glanced at Adam, who appeared to be enthralled, or even a little in shock. I reminded myself that we'd been reading applications and drinking wine for nearly three hours.

I dipped and raised the photograph, testing it against the lamp light. She was thinner, not as pretty as Alison, not as alert, Alison as she might appear if born under different circumstances. But yes, the applicant did bear a striking resemblance to our beloved Alison.

I read her responses to Adam's questions, all of which proved unremarkable, until I got to the "Final Comments" section on the last page of her application:

Dear Sir, six months ago TJ and I were making plans to get married. During my blood test they found abnormalities. They did more tests and told me I have a rare disease with no cure and that I had one year. I guess that leaves me six months give or take. TJ cried like a baby and came by the next day to tell me he couldn't take it. That was the last time I saw him.

So why is this dying person applying to be your wife? Good question. This sounds stupid but my sister Lynn saw you at the mall and picked up a flier and application. She showed me your picture and said you were my type. Not blood type, ha-ha. I'm no Vampire Lady. I guess I could of felt sorry for myself but I just laughed out loud being that laughter is the best medicine, right? It did help me lighten up and also took the pressure off Lynn. She said so you're going to do it? I said why not, I have no pride. And it's not like I'm going to meet you. If there was any chance of that happening you think I would be doing this?

Anyway Mr. Adam Tyne I'm done. You can stick a fork in me but don't take it the wrong way. I'm not that kind of girl. No really all goofing aside. Good luck finding a nice wife. I'm sure you deserve it.

Terri V ☺

I placed Terri's final comments and photo on the table. Adam picked up the photo and studied it awhile. His face seemed to wither and grow pale as I watched him. A tear was forming in my eye, threatening to roll down my cheek. I discretely wiped it away. We both pretended this was all manageable. We tried our best to spare one another. I put my hand on Adam's shoulder. He nodded and took a deep breath.

There was no way out. Call it fate or whatever. Adam was going to marry Terri V. We both knew it, just as we knew he would bury her within the year. Neither of us harbored any illusions on that front.

Winter 2015

DURING WINTER BREAK, when Sophie is at work, the house becomes too big for me. After a lackluster workout and hot shower, I drive to the mall and putter about, looking younger than my years, and somewhat distinguished and mysterious.

I'm not saying this to boast. It happens to be true. I sense bored middle-aged women squeezing me into their cluttered minds, entertaining what-ifs in the midst of spraying perfume samples on their wrists, and lifting pretty blouses in the air to visualize themselves wearing them. Would they gather to sing *Happy Birthday, Dear Francis,* if I announced that I had turned fifty-nine today?

In the sporting goods shop, I sit on an exercise machine and flex confidently though, admittedly, I'm pulling weight more suitable for prepubescent boys and menopausal women than for men. At this stage of life, there's no catching Carson Stackey, is there?

A young male employee coaches me through some strength exercises, while a blonde in a short pixie haircut looks over at me at least three times while curling dumbbells. I am dazzled by the whiteness of her smile, and the size of her biceps and thighs.

I'm tempted to shout, *I'm old enough to be your dad,* but the irony of being married to a much younger woman stops me. Instead, I grant Blondie of the big biceps and equally formidable thighs, a cordial nod and venture out into the main mall corridor.

The scent of stir-fried meats and veggies tickles my olfactory glands and turns to water on my tongue. I need food. I need to eat. I am fully aware that things could be worse, much worse. My chest swells as I inhale my good fortune. I am a respected and popular professor at the university, and winner of the 2005 Broderick Simeon Outstanding Professor of the Year Award. I enjoy overall good health, a gorgeous young wife, a solid portfolio, three wonderful daughters, beautiful grandchildren, and a miracle baby on the way. What right have I to grumble about anything?

Blondie motors past me, smiling so whitely and waving so fervently, that I am left feeling she has a stake in whatever enterprise I am willing to undertake.

Age really is a state of mind. I'm one-hundred percent certain of it when I order Mongolian Barbecue, watch the Eurasian princess pile my plate extra high, and hear her say, "Here you are, handsome," as she reaches over the counter and hands me the plate.

But no, actually... No, that is *not* what she said. She said, "Here you are, *sir*?" like a question, in that peculiar way some people talk, as if perpetually begging indulgence.

I shake my head and laugh. I'm laughing at myself, of course, but the look on her face, the uneasy stare, the faint tensing of her body jolt me into self-awareness. She thinks I'm mocking her. She thinks I'm a misogynistic oaf.

I immediately reset my tone and demeanor. "Thank you, ma'am," I say, nodding respectfully.

Did I just say *ma'am*?

To distract her, I tell her today is my birthday, number 59. She seems confused for a moment, but then her face lights up. She reaches under the counter and draws out a small packet containing an *Original Mongolian Black Truffle*. I watch her delicate hand reach over the counter and place the truffle in my hand.

"Happy Birthday, sir!" she sings in a sweet high voice.

And then I am alone again, seated in a corner that offers a panoramic view and allows for uninterrupted introspection. Eating alone in a mall food court, surrounded by a few strangers and the muted buzz of activity, has a way of stimulating memory and imagination, for better or worse.

Winter 1992

I GOT HOME LATE. I was dog-tired. The girls were asleep upstairs. Before leaving for work, I had reminded Kate that I had promised one of my former students I would go see him play with the varsity basketball team. It was a special occasion. He told me he had been promoted to first-string point guard, and said I had a lot to do with that. Apparently, I had once said something in class that had motivated him, and changed his life around.

"Don't ever give up on people, and don't ever give up on yourself."

I don't remember saying that.

I got home, sat at the kitchen table, and sipped cognac. Kate came down from upstairs, drifted into the kitchen, and sat across from me. She asked me about the game and then grew silent for a while. Then, in a strange voice, she asked me about Oliver Benedict, Chairman of the English Department. How was Dr. Benedict doing? How was his young wife, the Russian lady? Benedict's first wife died a year ago, and he remarried six months later.

"Outwardly, he seems fine," I said. "As far as Emma Petrov? I've yet to meet her. My understanding is that her family left Russia at the start of the Bolshevik revolution, lost a fortune, and settled in Paris... Is there something you want to tell me, Kate?"

"Adam's going to stop by."

"Tonight?"

"He wants to speak to you. He's leaving for California."

"I understand that, but why tonight? He said he wasn't leaving until next week. Can we reschedule?"

She didn't answer my question. She went to the kitchen sink and ran water. I listened to the water, and thought how clean everything looked. I walked into the living room. The hardwood floor had never been shinier. Everything, for the first time that I could remember, was in its place. Everything looked perfect.

Within a half hour, Adam appeared at the door looking pale and anxious. His eyes had a bruised cavernous quality. Terri V's death had ruined him. He had lost a good deal of weight and seemed to be caving inward, as though his bones had begun to disintegrate. I made

14

an effort to surmount my selfish impulses and asked him to have a seat in the living room. I offered him a drink, but he shook his head.

"Are the girls in bed?" he whispered.

"Yes, they are."

"Oh, okay."

"Adam, what's going on?"

I tried to smile. I thought, at the least, I should project a certain confidence and strength for the three of us, but fatigue and a restless stomach were betraying me.

"It's been a long day, pal," I said.

Adam glanced at Kate, who had seated herself to my right on the couch, and who appeared utterly deflated.

"Adam?" I said.

He took a deep unsteady breath and tried, but failed, to maintain eye contact with me. His eyes grew leaden and his head dipped. He gazed at my feet, as though seeking in them a way forward, and he said, "After Terri..."

But he could not finish. What could he not tell me? That I should have dissuaded him from contacting Terri V? Or was it something more primal? My good fortune? My children? My wife? I gazed at him with pity, love, and anger. I wanted to slap his face and yell at him, *No more stupid love games!*

But I could not do it. My arm went limp. I looked away, disgusted with myself, for I too had bought into the scheme. I too had allowed a pretty face to lead us all deeper into calamity.

Oh, Terri, sweet girl, forgive us.

"Damn it, Adam, I'll always be your brother," I avowed. "Do you hear me?"

Adam's eyes welled with tears. I wanted to go to him, make it all right, but some force kept me from standing.

"I was home Monday trying to get organized," he said. "I began to remember them, Terri and Alison. God, it was like someone started to pump air out of the room. I started gasping. I thought I was going to suffocate. I ran out into the street so I could breathe. I should have kept running. Why did I come *here*? Why did Kate open the door?"

He covered his mouth and nose with his hands, as if he were about to sneeze, and stared at the floor, looking stunned.

Then, without warning, he pleaded, "Forgive us. Please forgive us."

I glanced in confusion at Kate. She was leaning back against the couch. Her eyes were closed. Her arms were crossed over her chest, as if to protect her heart.

Forgive us?

Who did he mean by *us*? Adam and Alison? Adam and Terri? Adam and...?

My mind slipped, and I began to fall from a great height, glimpsing the unthinkable and bracing myself for the terrible collision.

But wait, how could this be? No, this was bullshit of the highest order. Crazy sick bullshit from hell.

I had *not* glimpsed anything. I had *not* understood anything. All I understood, me, Francis Clavel, was lectures, theses, term papers, how to improve poorly developed themes, how to correct bad writing and head-scratching leaps of logic. How to minister to ignorance.

But this? I had *not* understood *this*. Forgive *us*?

Now settle down. Why assume the worst? Your thinking is wrong. A clarification is pending, an explanation. At worst, we are dealing with a healthy dose of embarrassment. And Kate being mortified. Kate distancing herself, and any moment now, standing up and smiling awkwardly, asking if anyone wants coffee, pretending this gross misunderstanding never happened.

Adam looked so thin. His fingers were like crooked sticks. And Kate gave no indication she was about to get up and make coffee. Had she stopped breathing?

I was sinking deep into the cold, black silence, drowning. I reached for something to hold and clutched at the wild notion that we were engaged in a strange fantasy. We were roleplaying, in fact, and it was my turn to move the scene forward. I glanced at the burning red digits on the cable box clock: 10:59.

My flesh was numb and tingly as I stood up. I walked toward Adam and paused to examine his stick fingers. Did he feel numb and tingly too? From the corner of my eye, I could see Kate. She seemed to be shrinking.

I walked back to the couch, my bones softening, life oozing out of me with an odor of surrender. I sank into the cushion, blind and mute, dispatched to a distant place, unable to press the matter. All was lost. Past, present, future. Everything that ever was, forever lost.

But what was this? Kate sobbing?

"No, you don't get to do this!" I shouted as I jumped up. "You don't get to be the victim!" I leaned forward and whispered, " *You* killed us. You killed us all."

I glanced at Adam and gestured weakly to the door. "Go, just go."

A terrible silence followed. Then Kate began to sob ever so softly, as if murmuring a lullaby. "Oh, Francis," she gasped suddenly, and the sharp, slippery blade of love sliced open my heart. In a blur, I went out the front door and drove away.

Winter 1993

KATE AND THE GIRLS stayed in the house, of course, and I moved into a small apartment near campus. Dr. Benedict called me into his office one day. He told me he was revisiting Fitzgerald's *Tender Is the Night*, which he found to be a *deliciously maddening* read.

"Those complicated souls with their complicated lives," he said with a probing eye.

Was that the reason he had summoned me? To discuss *Tender Is the Night*?

I nodded, yes, *complicated souls*.

After staring at me for a while, he got to the point. "Divorce can be like a death in the family, Francis. But, of course, it all depends on how we manage life going forward."

He invited me to *open up*. I told him I was fine, all things considered. I was in *adjustment mode*, I said with an unconvincing smile. He withheld judgment and invited me to dinner, assuring me Emma would be glad to finally meet me.

Nine years at the English Department, and not once had Kate and I been invited to the Benedict residence by Oliver and his late wife, Eleanor.

I felt like a charity case, but out of respect, I accepted the invitation. A nameless, middle-aged woman served us dinner, dessert and coffee, and then vanished without speaking a single word.

Emma said she was reading *Tender Is the Night* for the first time, but expressed no opinion about it. Oliver offered unique insights into the novel's primary characters, Dick and Nicole Diver, and Rosemary Hoyt, and carefully considered my guarded responses to his remarks.

Overall, a pleasant evening, delicious food and fine wine. On my way out, Oliver grabbed me by the arm and informed me he and Emma agreed it would be wonderful if I had dinner with them again. Why not every other Saturday, circumstances permitting?

I was flattered, as well as apprehensive. I had mixed feelings about this unexpected proposition, but I was a lonely man in desperate need of purpose and direction. Dinner with the Benedicts had been easy enough, and more of these encounters might prove therapeutic, and even beneficial for my career and novel-writing aspirations.

My colleague, Mitch Kincaid, having gotten wind of our dinners, pulled me aside one day. He speculated in an oblique way about the Benedicts' motives, made references to *Anna Karenina* and cryptic allusions to Emma Petrov's exotic nature and Tsarist roots.

I listened, fascinated, humoring Mitch, who many in the department felt should have retired at least five years ago.

During one of those biweekly dinners, while Oliver was taking a call in his study, Emma confided that her husband was quite fond of me, and that he would be submitting my name for the Broderick Simeon Outstanding Professor of the Year Award. She seemed dead serious.

By then, I had already caught glimpses of Emma's arrogance, particularly during certain exchanges with her housekeeper. And so, though I might have found her claim flattering a few weeks ago, I now felt she was testing me, playing a mind game.

I was the youngest tenured professor in the English Department. Did that make me an easy target? I remembered what Professor Kincaid had said about Emma. In response to her remark, I asked her how she had found Oliver. Not how they had met, but how she had found him, in the way one might find a pot of gold, for example.

Her eyes pierced me. She turned away in what seemed to me at the time a gesture of wounded forbearance. She walked out of the room, pretending the old man had called her. "What is it, Oliver, dear? I could not hear what you said."

Emma was an accomplished pianist. She liked to play nocturnes after dinner while her polymath husband spoke at length on wide-ranging subjects, from the Western literary canon to the great works of architecture, to the manufacturing of purple dye and the discovery of glassblowing. Oliver's voice was like an accompanying instrument to Emma's piano. She often closed her eyes, swaying dreamily as her hands moved over the keys.

One Saturday, I arrived for dinner as usual. Emma explained, with an abstracted air, that her husband had been called away, but that he had insisted I stay to keep her company. The housekeeper served dinner and disappeared.

We ate slowly, savoring the silence with the same restrained pleasure we took chewing the mouthwatering slivers of Beef Wellington that had been placed before us.

"Oliver has gone to London," she said. She glanced to the side and stared as if spellbound, as if before her eyes some inanimate thing were trembling into life.

Later she played the piano with cool detachment, ignoring me, and leading me to almost believe she missed her husband. I watched her carefully, her every movement like wine to my thirsting tongue. When she finished, she got up and stared at me with seductive contempt. I followed her up the stairs to a spacious candlelit bedroom. She said, "This is not complicated. It is not about Oliver, whatever you may think. It is about nothing at all."

I was thinking along the same lines. This was not complicated. It was not about Kate or anything at all, really. Or so I told myself.

In the midst of feverish kisses and groping, I froze. She eyed me with a curious smile and assured me Oliver would have no issue with what we were doing, if that was my concern. It had been his idea after all, she said, and that was why she loved him.

I told her I could not play her game, and I left. I declined subsequent invitations that arrived regularly in my mailbox, and I avoided Oliver as much as possible. Whenever our paths crossed, and the exchange of a word was unavoidable, Oliver seemed surprised, as if we had stumbled upon one another in a foreign land.

Spring 2015

AT FIVE IN THE MORNING, I learn that the baby has a cleft lip. Sophie knew but never told me. Did she think I wouldn't notice?

"Who in your family has a cleft lip?" I ask wearily.

"I don't know."

"What did you say?"

"I don't know."

"No one on my side," I point out.

He is a beautiful baby boy, nonetheless, and a cleft lip is better than a cleft palate, or a cleft lip *and* a cleft palate.

"Let's name him Francis," Sophie whispers.

"No, not Francis, he's a Rick," I reply, enlisting Sophie's dad, who no one has heard from in two years.

At 9:00 AM, Dr. Clark says he prefers *Rick* over *Francis*, and assures us he has seen far worse cases of cleft lip. "No worries. In due time, Rick will be clamping onto Mommy's teat and giving it a nice shake with no problem whatsoever," he offers crudely.

I should be offended by Dr. Clark's demeanor and choice of words. I suppose I am, in a semidetached way. I glance at my mother-in-law, Onora, who is nodding in agreement with the doctor.

"You'll be using this special needs, long nipple bottle for a while," says the doctor, but I'm barely listening, having moved on to greater concerns.

Like Rick's nose, ears, and mouth. What about eye color? Too soon to tell. And the pink yellowish complexion? Jaundice. Poor kid exits the womb into a world that has presented him a cleft lip, jaundice, and a daddy who, presently, is too preoccupied to be overcome with love and joy.

Sophie is too drained to pretend anything. I look over at Mrs. Kaminski, who is alluring in a pale, meaty way. I'm wondering if I'll be around when Sophie gets like that. I don't think she will, not if her knees hold up and she keeps running six miles a day. She'll be looking good for a while, for someone else, long after I'm gone.

"So, who does the baby look like, Onora?" I ask, trying to sound playful. "Your husband?"

"Oh no, not that one, no, no," she assures me, shaking her head. "Oh no, uh-uh." She draws close and peers deep into my eyes, as if seeking the answer to a big question. Then she turns away, looking disgusted.

Late afternoon, Carson Stackey shows up unannounced with Mel, his wife. Brief, awkward banter is interrupted by a new nurse. She sees Stackey, and as bubbly as can be, steps up to him and says, "Congratulations, Daddy!"

Taken aback for an instant, Stackey recovers enough to force a fake laugh. I follow suit. Our laughs converge like raging tributaries, forming one manly river of loud ugly laughter.

"Mr. Clavel, please accept my apologies," the nurse says, realizing her error. "I just assumed, which I shouldn't have, obviously, but I..."

"Oh, not at all, no need to apologize, Leslie," I say, glancing at her nametag. "I can see why you might think that."

"I am *so* sorry, sir."

"No, not at all, and no need to refer to me as *sir*, ma'am," I blurt out.

It strikes me like never before that I don't really know Sophie. A brief awkward silence ensues, but Stackey comes to the rescue, reminding everyone Sophie needs her rest. Good old Stackey. We shake hands with rough force, and I can't take my eyes off that misaligned mustache that conceals his cleft lip.

Mel's little fish of a hand slips in and out of my palm. "Nice to see you too," she replies blandly.

Mrs. Kaminski accompanies the Stackeys out of the room. "I'm getting coffee," she says, glancing back. "Can I get you coffee, Francis?"

"No, thank you, Mom," I say with a wink. She shakes her head, feigning annoyance. Onora and I are about the same age. We get along great, have a common understanding about life's pitfalls. And my darling Sophie? Well, Sophie Mom is trying to will herself to sleep. Sometimes I think Sophie and I are two distinct life forms wandering in vastly different worlds.

When Onora comes back, I tell her I'm going to run down to get some coffee. She gives me a look and waves her hand as if she's getting ready to spank my bottom. This is what we do, and why she likes me.

On my way to the elevator, I stop outside the nursery to get another look at Rick. Through the glass wall, I see a tiny bundle of motionless life. I read *Clavel* in marker blue at the foot of the incubator. For a moment, I become confused and lightheaded. I place both hands on the glass to steady myself. *Clavel*, that's my surname, right?

Nurse Leslie walks past holding a clipboard. I follow her. I would like information on performing a paternity test, I want to say. She stops and turns around, and my mouth opens, but no words come out. I force a smile. Finally, I say, "What you said before. That was very funny, you know."

Nurse Leslie smiles politely, nods, and continues on her rounds.

○ ○ ○ ○ ○

RICK IS A WORLD CHANGER. In the sense that he changes how those around him perceive and engage the world. Now the same can be said of any baby Rick, and there are too many baby Ricks in the world to count in a single episode, and you would think, given their vast numbers and the soothing effect their presence has on those graced with a soul, that the world would be a kinder place.

At three months, Rick undergoes surgery to repair the cleft lip. It is clear the boy is champing at the bit to lock his little mouth onto Sophie's teat.

Doctor Clark says, "Rick's almost there. Let's help him out with a little simulation exercise. Try this for ten days." He hands me a special syringe with a soft rubber feeding tube.

The boy is growing nicely and rapidly, and I find myself trapped in fatherhood limbo. I'm restless. I get annoyed easily.

For example, Sophie doesn't want to go back to work until she fully weans the boy, which could take up to twenty-four months.

"Twenty-four months?" I say.

"A mother's colostrum is perfect food."

"I understand about the colostrum, but what about your job?"

"What about it?"

"Didn't you tell Stocky you'd be back in six months?"

"*Stackey*, not *Stocky*. Oh, uh, I didn't tell you. We talked."

"You and Stocky."

"Carson, yes. We talked last week. He said whenever I'm ready..."

"Ready for what?"

"Excuse me?"

"Ready to leave Rick? Is that what you're getting ready to do?"

"Wait a second, Francis. Weren't you the one getting bent out of shape about me being out of work for twenty-four months?"

"I am not getting bent out of shape. And the number of months is not the issue."

"So, are you saying you don't want me to go back to work at all?"

"That is *not* the question that is foremost on my mind."

"God, Francis, I don't understand you at all."

She grabs Rick out of the crib and carries him down the stairs. I want to shout something nasty at her, but I check myself.

I go down to my study. A stack of term papers is sitting on my desk in judgment of me. *No, not now, I can't do you*, I tell it. I head to the bathroom, splash water on my face, and watch the water swirl down the basin drain.

I'm getting too old for this, I remind myself, and I hear a tiny whimper. Sophie is standing behind me, and she's holding Rick. Okay, so there's something she needs to get off her chest, but she's not sure how to begin, so I take the lead.

"The Stackeys, your boss and his wife, Mel? I don't remember hearing about children."

"She can't have kids," Sophie says after a slight hesitation. We go to the kitchen, put Rick in his bouncy chair, and flip the *On* switch to mild vibration.

Sophie takes what's left of a chocolate cake she baked a couple of days ago out of the refrigerator and spoons a generous portion into her mouth. Her features soften noticeably. Her mood is altered. I'm encouraged. She swallows and licks the spoon on both sides and studies the faded streaks her tongue has left on the smooth stainless steel. Her gaze drifts up to the right. She's contemplating something she may or may not want to share with me.

After a long silence, I pointlessly ask, "Why do you use a spoon to eat cake?"

She ignores me and eats more cake, chewing in an open, enticing manner that reveals her chocolate-flavored tongue in all its splendor. She licks her lips and then the spoon, fully aware of the effect her little show is having on me. Her tongue licks both sides of the spoon with devotional attentiveness, and as the licking expands, my own mouth fills with water.

When I have forgotten everything but her siren's mouth, she jolts me with a dose of crazy schoolgirl laughter.

"Sometimes Rick looks just like you when you get that bedazzled Francis Clavel look," she says, making everything seem perfect.

Rick is sleeping. We go upstairs and bring him along in his vibrating bouncy chair, hoping he'll remain asleep for at least a half hour.

Summer 2015

I SPRINT THE LAST hundred yards of my two-mile jog, stop on the front lawn, hands on knees, panting like I have just completed a marathon. Some days I miss Kate terribly. Today is one of those days. I scoop the plastic-wrapped newspaper up off the turf and remember Sophie, and that we haven't made love since the chocolate spoon episode over a month ago. Am I at fault? Yes, I think so.

I sense movement. Sophie is walking away from the big bay window and back into the darkened interior of our home. Can she read my heart? Can she see how much I miss Kate today?

Over the years my daughters have kept me abreast of things. Chuck Mills is nothing like a Clavel, they tell me, but they have grown to love him. They love me more, of course, there's no comparison, but they love him too, in a different way, like an uncle. Chuck owns a car dealership. He played right tackle, second team, at Ohio State. He is a huge benevolent bear. I know firsthand, having encountered him at graduations, weddings, baptisms, and so on.

And Kate...

Kate has, for the most part, maintained her youthful figure. Her face has changed. Or perhaps it changes only when I see her. Or when she sees me. I think—no, I *know*—it is a face no one else can see or will ever see, the one I alone can see, the one that reveals to me my own face, that is, *our* face, marked with our past joys and sorrows and disfigured by our unspoken, unlived life.

That said, Kate seems quite well. She is active in church and community. We haven't had a real conversation since the divorce. Now and then we exchange family-related details by phone or during unavoidable gatherings. She is kind to my wife, and I am kind to her husband. Our hellos and goodbyes are always cordial.

Years ago, during our grandson Justin's third birthday party, Kate and I coincided in Lisa's kitchen. We commented on the new cabinets, the granite countertop. Nothing, really, just the things people who rarely see each other talk about. As Kate began to walk back to the living area, I feared I might never have another opportunity. I called her name. She stopped, but did not look back. I apologized for the terrible things I said to her that awful night. She seemed to be pondering my words, and how her response could mark the end of an unfinished chapter.

But why respond at all? And why had I put her in this awkward position? I should have kept my mouth shut. But to my relief, she turned and gazed at me without the slightest trace of recrimination or satisfaction. She nodded sweetly, gracing me with her gentlest smile, and returned to her husband.

Her husband. Not me, the other man. I sometimes imagine big Chuck eclipsing like the moon, his departure opening an opportunity for me, but then I curse myself. I curse my selfish soul.

I need a shower, but first I'll check on Sophie. I find her upstairs in Rick's room. She looks exhausted. Rick's eyes are half-closed. I take him from her and kiss his smooth milky forehead.

"I'm going to put him down for a nap," I whisper.

"Lisa called," Sophie says in her most fragile voice.

And somehow, I know. Of course, I know. I know as surely as I know I have been blessed beyond understanding for the years Kate and I shared together, for our three daughters and our grandchildren, and yes, for Sophie and Rick.

"Francis, Lisa called."

"Yes, Lisa called, uh-huh."

"It's about Kate."

"I know, sweetheart."

○ ○ ○ ○ ○

I HAVE OFTEN IMAGINED Adam driving up and down the freeway in a silver Porsche wearing a blank expression, and his latest conquest sitting in the passenger seat talking to herself.

Time portions out loss with no measure of equity. At too young an age Adam lost Alison, then Terri V. Then he lost Kate and me. Not by choice. We lost one another. Some nefarious spirit, a demon from hell, killed who we once were.

At the wake, Lisa pulls me aside. She has given the world three handsome boys, the oldest a gifted high school freshman who wants to be a scientist. Her husband, Hunter, is an accountant. When he sees me, he goes out of his way to assure me Hunter Junior reminds him of me. The eyes, he says, though not the eyes themselves, but their way of seeing. I don't know why he says this, or exactly what he means. I don't ask him to elaborate. He means well, but he tries too hard, and I'm not totally sure why he always seems less than comfortable with me. Do I remind him of a former English teacher?

I look at Hunter Junior as he stares at the floor. He seems far away. His brothers, seated next to him, are incapable of being still. Hunter's eyes are dry and clear. Such eyes can see over great distances, can see light years away. Maybe that's what my son-in-law is trying to get at. Hunter Junior can see far into the future. He's a visionary. And me, Francis Clavel? I'm nearing sixty, and I too can see far. I see far and deep into the past. I am a retrovisionary.

Big Chuck is a sorry sight. I can't help wondering if he has a greater capacity for love than I. He had more years to love Kate. Did she love him more than me?

Amazing how calm and collected Lisa appears standing beside me. I feel her waiting patiently for me to complete my reveries.

"Are you all right, sweetie?" I ask her.

"I'm fine, Dad. There's someone out in the hall who wants to see you."

How I dread these unsolicited encounters. I'm in no mood to indulge individuals I haven't thought about in decades, or whose names I've forgotten, or whom I thought were dead and buried.

But Lisa, like her mother, is irresistibly lovely in her earnestness. I acquiesce and am led to a hallway where a balding, whitehaired man in black sits in profile on a bench staring at his folded hands. He rises tentatively when he becomes aware of me.

Perplexed, I turn looking for Lisa. But she has abandoned me, leaving me at the mercy of this stranger, who walks toward me, his head bowed. Is this the prophet of my imminent demise?

Ho! Is that a Roman collar? My throat constricts, and my mind is darkened by the vast shadow of my many sins. For the love of God, whose idea was this? I clear my throat as I take a step back, impelled by some primal instinct to run from such figures. But the voice arrests me.

"Francis."

It is a familiar voice that opens the floodgates of memory and, after an instant of fear, draws me across a peaceful meadow. His voice is like a bell of regeneration, calling me home from the dark forest.

"Adam?"

A funeral home attendant stops in the hall to watch us embrace and exchange unrehearsed words of reconciliation. We take a step back, and regard each other with a touch of sadness. Will the memory of this extraordinary encounter be our lasting gift to one another?

I lead him to Kate. He gazes at her grim taut face, that somehow remains beautiful, despite the mortician's indifferent hand. Adam's own expression grows peaceful and confident as he lowers himself onto the velvet kneeler before the casket to pray for Kate's soul.

Adam is a father too, finally. Father Adam. Did I ever doubt it? I watch him pray to the God of the inscrutable and the imperfect, and I realize how dissimilar Adam and I are. I cannot pray to God as he does. I do not hear God's voice. I feel no divine prompting, nor inspiration. I see no visions.

I whisper in the darkness, *God, can you hear me?*

After the burial, I think it best to forgo the gathering at the Mills' residence. I hug Chuck, who breaks into loud sobs while in my arms. I shake hands with *their* son and kiss *their* daughter. My heart races at their unexpected familiarity. Something of her, of Kate, endures. Their aura, their eyes, something precious and inescapably *mine*.

Adam embraces and blesses me. Father, Son, Holy Spirit. I take his hand. I want more than a priest. I want my friend. He kisses my hand, and then he is gone.

I worry about Virginia. I encourage her, tell her how proud I am of her. She looks at me with benign skepticism. Did Kate ever tell the girls what happened with us? Did she tell anyone?

"I love you," I say. "I love you so much, sweetie."

And poor Irene, pregnant and exhausted, beleaguered by little ones and burdened by an unreliable husband.

"How I love you, my angel," I tell her.

She manages a smile, hugs me hard and wipes a tear from her cheek. Lisa walks me to my car. She is the one most like her mother. I am tempted to ask her, *Did Mom ever tell you why we divorced?* But my lips remain pressed together. She hands me an envelope. "It's from Mom," she says.

The moment takes my breath away, and my heart becomes a deep bell tolling the unknown terrors of love. Lisa holds me for a long time, passing on her inherited strength. Then she watches me drive off, like a concerned mother sending her child off to school for the first time. In the rearview mirror, I see her blow me a kiss, wave good-bye, and turn away suddenly. Goodbye, Lisa, my darling.

At home Sophie is breastfeeding sleepy-eyed Rick.

"How is he?" I say.

"He's better. The fever's down. I'm sorry I couldn't be there with you, Francis."

"I know. It's alright, darling. You were where you needed to be."

Later, while Sophie and the baby sleep, I walk out to the backyard to count stars, and to pray: "Before I die, I think I should know the truth. But I can't bring myself to ask her. You know what a coward I am. Please, help me."

Fall 2016

TIME PASSES. I can't bring myself to read Kate's letter.

Rick is walking. He's a strong and alert little boy, and unbearably sweet. The sight of him breaks my heart a thousand times a day. Sophie is fit again. And I am not. I have stopped running. I no longer work out. I have lost muscle mass and my appetite. I don't sleep well. I shave once every ten days, or so.

I lack ambition. I am shortchanging my students. I scribble clichés on their papers. My memory plays cruel tricks on me.

I grow old, I grow old...

Sophie thinks it would be nice to adopt a little girl so that Rick can have a sister. She becomes cold and withdrawn when I fail to react in any way.

I wonder if I will ever read Kate's letter. I carry it with me everywhere I go. It has become a part of me, as critical to my functioning as a heart valve.

Will I ever find the courage to open it?

○ ○ ○ ○ ○

IT IS A BEAUTIFUL SATURDAY MORNING. A man roughly my age collapses on the sidewalk outside the municipal library while trying to board a bus. He dies before the ambulance arrives, leaving those of us present shaken like orphans.

There is a faint smell of aftershave lotion in the air. What looks like a small mole on his chin is, in fact, a pimple of dried blood. Had he had any premonition, any reason to think he had shaved for the last time this morning? A couple of us stay until the ambulance carries his body away, as though in conformity with some unwritten code. We are silent witnesses at the gates of eternity.

In a deserted corner of the library, obscured like a shadow, I read Kate's letter. It begins with the words, *Francis, my love and my life.*

○ ○ ○ ○ ○

SOPHIE CLAVEL KAMINSKI.

So touchingly beautiful, holding Rick in her arms.

Have you been weeping? my silent heart asks.

"Sophie? What is it?"

"It's Rick."

My heart begins to thump, but the boy appears as healthy and robust as ever. His plump little legs kick out fiercely, and his Popeye arms reach for me with desperate vigor. My face breaks into smile.

31

"Puh-puh-puh."

"He's been saying that all morning," Sophie says, her mouth twisting with emotion. "He looks for you. He wants his Papa."

She presses her lips against his cheek and closes her eyes.

"Is that correct, Mister Rick, what your mom said?"

"Puh-puh."

"Oh, Francis," Sophie moans, and for a timeleaping instant, her lament and Kate's become one. I take Rick from her and sit on the sofa. I swing him up over my head repeatedly, each thrust celebrated with a lusty *Ho!*

The daredevil in Rick cannot get enough of this. He shrieks in delight each time I hoist him up into the air. Sophie sidles next to me on the sofa and begins to weep. She presses her face against my chest and sinks her nails into my ribs and stomach.

And for this, I am eternally grateful.

The witnesses have gathered. I see them standing by the opposite wall, Kate and Adam and Alison and Terri V, the four of them watching and listening.

"I thank the God of beautiful sorrows," I say aloud.

The words echo in my mind as I pull away and get on one knee before my wife. I prop Rick on my left thigh. With my free hand, I paint Sophie's new day, spreading her tears across her flushed cheeks with my fingers.

She stops weeping. She watches me uncertainly. She waits.

But who am I to judge? Who is anyone?

And kisses are always better than words.

I kiss the warm tremulous almonds that are her eyes. One, and then the other. I press my lips to her lips, gently but surely, like a physician taking a pulse, like a pilgrim discovering new life.

Where Are You, Ricardo?

THE SWAN GLIDED over the black water like a big, beautiful wound-up toy. Joseph felt the quiet rippling motion of the water inside him, as if it were his blood that rippled. The cob was performing the obligatory response to bread-tossing with gorgeous mechanical precision. Joseph understood the state of Ricardo's mind but had no reason to like it.

"This business suck, Ricardo," he said shaking his head.

Farther back, against a backdrop of monochrome reeds and willows floated the female, her feathers withered and lusterless. The gusts pushed her this way and that like a lifeless thing whose sole purpose was to trouble the living. Her decline had come as suddenly as the November winds.

Joseph broke off more pieces of bread and flung them at the lake. The cob plucked and gulped, plucked, and gulped. To Joseph's eye, the same slate sky that suppressed the female's anima coaxed from the cob's interior a consternating luminosity.

He never believed that swans sang before they died. There were no swan songs other than those sung by delirious men and women.

Having tired of the old man's largesse, the cob drifted back to within a few feet of its mate and adopted her resigned disposition, and their lifeless trajectories were governed by the capricious wind. Joseph squatted on the bank and reached into the icy water. With wet fingers he crossed himself and formulated words that would remain unspoken, for what could he say to the bird that he hadn't already said?

He climbed the slick lumpy path back up to the bridge that split the lake and the retirement village and walked across it. In April he had ventured through the reeds in search of the nest, but the apoplectic cob had erupted suddenly from a thicket of cattails and sedges, coming within inches of taking a bite out of his rear end.

Despite the regrettable encounter there were no lingering animosities. To Joseph's thinking, he and Ricardo had become cautiously comfortable in one another's presence. But there would be no babies this year and Lucy was dying.

Joseph returned to the 850 square foot ranch house with reluctance. He closed the front door behind him and entered the small living-dining combo area where Clara spent her days. In the usual manner, he paused to study the yellowing gray, grime-creased chairback, the worn stained wheels, Clara's furrowed neck. Too many years had passed since he'd last run his fingers through her once thick dark hair. The ashen, boyish head left him perched before a wasteland, his throat clogged with dust. He began to count from memory the number of beers in the refrigerator.

She was as he had left her, pushed against the table before a 25-inch tube television from another era. A nun with unblinking eyes stared at him from the TV monitor as she mouthed a near silent rosary. He stepped sideways to avoid the nun's scrutiny. From where he now stood, he could see Clara's and the nun's lips moving in synchronicity. With her good hand Clara rubbed one rosary bead after another between her fingers. How many damn rosaries could a person pray in one day? Joseph wondered as he cast his eye on the frayed duct tape wrapped around the wheelchair's left armrest.

"Randy need change," he said as he approached the birdcage.

He stuck a thick calloused finger through the cage bars. The parakeet assaulted the finger, biting and pecking ferociously. Joseph enjoyed the parakeet's rage.

"You hear me, Clara? Randy need change."

"You don't need to shout!"

"I no shout. How I know you hear me?"

"I ain't hard of hearing, Joseph."

He got in front of her and said, "You say you no hard of hearing. Okay, you say so. But you hard in da head." He poked the side of his head with his three middle fingers three times to drive home the point.

Clara snatched the remote control and turned the volume way up. The nun roared, "Blest art thou amongst women, and blest is the fruit of thy womb..."

"Ah, gah-damn, Clara! You make me go deaf."

Clara used her good hand to pull away from the table, rolling the big left wheel backwards in spastic arcs and jerking her torso until her back was to him and she was facing the front door. Joseph lunged for the remote control and shut off the TV.

"What you wanna prove, Clara?"

When she didn't respond he sighed.

"Why you say nothing when I come home? You no hear me come in?"

"I was praying."

"Even when you no pray. I come home you say nothing to me. How weather, Joseph? Joseph, how swan?"

"Randy wants fresh water," she said.

"So Randy, he tell you? You talk to Randy but not me?"

"I need to go to the bathroom."

Joseph rolled the wheelchair to the bathroom and helped Clara onto the toilet seat.

"No problem," he said. "You do your business. I take care of Randy."

He left her sitting on the toilet seat and changed the newspapers on the bottom of Randy's cage and poured fresh water into the little plastic trough and nudged a fresh piece of lettuce between the cage bars. When he got back to the bathroom Clara was bent over the sink like a broken mannequin. Her diaper was snagged on the metal bracing surrounding her right leg.

"Why you try get up?" Joseph said.

He replaced the diaper and pulled the wooly pink sweatpants back up over the bones that long ago were full round limbs and settled her back in the wheelchair.

"You get yourself killed, Clara," he said. "You gonna fall an hit head an kill yourself for gah-sake. You no get up without me no more, okay?"

He rolled her back to the table and took the remote control and clicked to a headline news channel. Then he went to the refrigerator and poured Clara a glass of apple juice and opened himself a beer and microwaved leftover noodles with Swedish meatballs and then sat down to eat lunch with his wife.

"Girl swan not looking too good," he said after a while.

Clara lifted the glass of juice to her mouth but placed the glass back on the table without drinking and stared at her husband who pretended to be distracted by a meatball.

She lifted the glass again and this time her hand began to shake and Joseph was poised to take the glass from her before she could make a mess, but she steadied herself and took a sip of the apple juice and placed the glass down without issue and wiped her thin bloodless lips with a paper napkin.

"Joseph, I wanna see the swans."

Every few days she said this, and each time Joseph responded with his standard objections.

"Big pain in ass, Clara. Root stick up everywhere. Go down slope an slide all over place, trip over root, get poison ivy, scratch face with torn, fall in lake."

"Bullshit."

"Clara, I tell you everything you wanna know about swan."

"Slope, my ass. You don't have to go down no stupid slope to see the swans."

"Male name Ricardo, okay? Female Lucy. They together long time. But no babies."

"Take me to see the swans. I never ask you for nothin', Joseph."

"You no ask me for nothing, huh? Ha. Okay. No ask because I give you everything maybe?"

He watched Clara shrink, but she recovered quickly and began yanking the left wheel with a vengeful fury, rotating the wheelchair counterclockwise toward the front door, always counterclockwise.

"Time no go backwards, Clara!" he shouted in anger that dissipated as suddenly as it had erupted.

He gazed at the homely chair back, the shriveled woman.

"Tell you what I do, Clara. I get you HDTV."

It took her some time to wheel herself back around toward him. Joseph waited patiently, respecting her new dignified air. She lifted her head and fixed her eyes on his.

"Soon, okay?" he said. "I get you HDTV soon."

"What does *soon* mean? How soon?"

"Soon, Clara, soon. You wan I get dictionary so you see what *soon* mean?"

"You're full of shit, Joseph."

"Oh, dat nice, Clara. I say I get you HDTV and you call me liar, you say I full of shit. Nice language for Catholic lady. What da hell wrong with you, Clara?"

"You got a secret stash of money hidden somewheres, Joseph? You're always whining about how ain't no money for this, ain't no money for that, blah, blah, blah."

"Blah, blah, blah. Dat good too. You intelligent woman, know how to say blah-blah-blah. Fine, you no believe me. Okay, Clara, no HDTV. Make you happy?"

"Soon like tomorrow?"

"I get good deal. Have to wait a little. Black Friday maybe, okay?"

Clara didn't say anything, which left Joseph feeling dissatisfied. He preferred Clara's insults to her silence, just as he preferred Randy's bites to his avian indifference. His rough hands gripped the wheelchair's worn rubber handles, and he positioned her in her usual spot against the table.

He changed the channel back to the Catholic station and nudged the cut cardboard square that held the thousand-piece *My Fair Lady* puzzle a little closer to Clara.

The puzzle was nearly completed. She had been working on it for several weeks. Last week Joseph noticed Audrey Hepburn was missing an eye and a chunk of face. Rex Harrison, on the other hand, was his smug whole self.

The piece wasn't missing. Clara had set it aside. Joseph could see it. How many times had he been tempted to complete Audrey's face when Clara wasn't looking? It was the kind of Clara detail that would have irritated him a few months ago, but all that had changed. One summer Friday had changed everything.

He washed the dishes and left them to dry in the broken dishwasher and changed his shoes and shirt and emptied his bladder and took the grocery list from beneath the parakeet magnet stuck to the refrigerator.

"Randy hate my gut," he said with a smile, but Clara pretended not to hear him as she studied the puzzle.

"I go to market. Tomorrow Saturday. We see how weather. Maybe I take you see swan tomorrow."

They both knew from the news that rain was heading their way, and Saturday would be a washout. Clara glanced at Randy, stiff and formal as a cadet, and at the young man on TV discussing *The Theology of the Body*, and again at Randy, and with each slow shift of her eyes, the faintest passing impression of Joseph's change of shoes and clean shirt stole breaths and blood from her.

He said, "I be back soon, okay Clara?"

Did she nod her assent? Yes, she did, he assured himself. He walked out of the tiny ranch house, turned the lock key and listened to the dead bolt slide into the shut position with a smooth oily thud.

THEY KNEW NOTHING about each other, but each found in the other an answer to a need. He liked to stand at the end of the aisle in front of the lycopene-rich jars of tomato sauce and paste, or saunter quietly by the boxes of rotini, capellini and angel hair as he listened for the click-clack of her high-heeled shoes on the tiled floor.

Often, she would silence her heels and pause nearby, out of sight, her ear attentive to the squeak of his imitation oxfords. They would sometimes look into each other's eyes as they pushed their shopping carts past each other, but sometimes not, one or the other feigning disinterest or distraction. Sometimes they would exchange bold, engaging smiles, and other times uncertain glances.

Close up, as they moved past each other, they witnessed the truth of their respective ages, but rather than disappoint, this knowledge encouraged and excited them, for each had defied the grind of time better than most.

Each viewed the other as accessible and discovered in the other a shared secret sensuality that teetered constantly on the brink of release. A mutual self-imposed silence, more suited to the monastery than the neighborhood supermarket, had purchased twelve Friday afternoon encounters and the illusion of impending intimacy.

She was full-figured and quite attractive for an older woman. She was Eleanor Parker, or someone that looked like her. Or the daughter of Eleanor Parker, when he did the math. Sometimes she was simply the woman who one day wore a summer dress that flowed like lake water over her curves. He thought of her as *Nora*, but he had no idea what her real name was.

When on the thirteenth Friday he found her in the canned goods aisle wearing stylish ankle boots, tight jeans and a short, fur-lined jacket (she was not yet aware of his presence, he didn't think), he took a deep, nervous breath.

What value was there in living a dead life? he often asked himself. Why should it be wrong to sow seeds of future happiness for oneself? Never as at that moment had he so adamantly rejected Ricardo's morbid acquiescence. But what could he say to Ricardo that would make a difference? His words meant less to Ricardo than bird droppings from the sky.

Joseph watched Nora roll a can of soup in her hands and imagined himself touching her forearm. A touch would redefine both their lives, he knew. It would be the key that opened the door to words, and words would open the door to mutual understanding, and understanding to intimacy...

But Clara could not know, not ever. Her ignorance was a mercy. He took good care of his Clara and would do so to the last breath, but how could he tell her that his days were made bearable by the existence of another woman? Clara was his wife, but did that mean he should die before his time along with her?

Joseph took several deep breaths, as though he were preparing to dive into a lake, and began to roll his shopping cart toward the woman. His shoes squeaked only ever so lightly, for he had directed his feet to move with dignity. But he could not keep his brain from engaging all manner of erotic fantasy.

At first, she did not recognize him, or pretended not to. He set the cart aside with a flourish and approached her with a smile and his right hand extended toward her, as if to lead her to a dance floor. The woman stared at Joseph for some moments with a troubled expression before retreating with her shopping cart in the opposite direction.

Joseph was baffled by her reaction. Wasn't this Nora?

He drew his head back to examine himself and was relieved to find his trousers free of stains, his fly zipped, and his hands clean. He touched his face, detected no drool, no crust, no foreign matter. What offense had he committed? He took a tentative step forward, his shoe letting out a plaintive squeak.

As if on cue Nora's retreat came to a sudden stop. She turned toward the shelves and grasped a packet of seasoned quick rice and twirled it to the ingredients label. He heard her say "Huh" and watched her place the packet in her cart as if it were an egg.

She lingered, looked down at her right foot, raised the tip of her boot to attention and moved it slowly in a circular clockwise motion pivoting off her heel. It was as if she had unstuck the boot from the floor and fashioned for Joseph a kind of sign language. He gleaned significance from the gesture, interpreting it as an exoneration of any wrongdoing on his part and as a veiled invitation. Bolstered by Nora's reconsideration of the matter, he pushed his shopping cart forward.

His happy progress was halted, however, by a pair of fluttering hands that drew his attention away from Nora's boot. Beyond the aisle's end, poised before *Meats*, a pear-shaped, jowly young woman in a bloodied white apron stood wiping her hands on her stomach and watching the interplay between Joseph and Nora.

Joseph paused thoughtfully, scratching his temple, and drew from his breast pocket the grocery list, the means by which he intended to extricate himself from the woman's gaze. He turned the shopping cart around and rolled to the opposite end of the aisle, glancing back once at Nora, who looked perplexed and miffed, no doubt interpreting his departure as a delayed retaliation to her initial snub. Someone started to laugh.

Nora gasped as she turned around and saw the laughing blood-stained woman.

Joseph, standing alone amid turkey and pilgrim paraphernalia in the *Seasonals* aisle, listened carefully to the remote giggles and snorts that might have nothing to do with him and Nora, or maybe everything. He listened for incriminating words. Every noise and silence sank him deeper into uncertainty.

When next he saw Nora, she was standing at the cash register emptying her cart. He gazed at her with longing, desiring only that she should remember him with a glance.

She turned her head just before leaving. Her smile was sweet and melancholic, reminiscent of the baroness's tender goodbye to von Trapp in *The Sound of Music*. Unlike von Trapp, there was to be no pretty Maria waiting for Joseph.

CLARA LIFTED HER HEAD to observe the Saturday news dangling from Joseph's hand like a dead quail. A triangle of dark spongy gray cut across the lower half of the newspaper. Joseph began to separate the pages and spread them out all over the living-dining room area to dry.

"We gotta talk, Joseph."

"No swan today, Clara. Rain all day."

"Not that."

She lowered her head and rubbed the rosary crucifix between her thumb and index finger, wearing away the corpus of the Christ.

"I go piss then we talk," Joseph said.

He looked for traces of Nora in the bathroom mirror. Would Clara piece together Nora's face when she looked at him? Would she hear the laughter of the *Meats* lady?

He splashed cold water on his face and rubbed his skin raw with a towel.

He stopped at Randy's cage on his way back to the table and poked his finger between the bars. The parakeet gave him no satisfaction and barely twitched its wings.

"What you wanna talk about, Clara? HDTV?"

Her mouth shaped a gentle melancholy as she gazed at the worn rosary crucifix. Joseph was reminded of Nora's parting smile and felt the irony like a cold hand clamped upon his neck.

Clara lifted her head.

"I worry, Joseph."

"Worry? You funny, Clara. What you worry for?"

"I worry about you."

"Me? Ha-ha. No need to worry for me, crazy woman."

"I worry about how you gonna be when I'm dead."

"What da hell you saying, Clara? Where dis come from? You gonna kill yourself? Is something you wanna say to me?"

She stared at him a long while. Who she once was flickered in her eyes the length of a deep breath before vanishing. Joseph's eyes widened as though someone had thrust a knife in his belly. Why this now? He was tired of chasing ghosts. Hadn't he had his fill of mourning? Nothing gonna change what we got now, who we are.

"Okay, Clara, you think about what you wanna say to me. I go get beer."

The rain was falling harder than he could ever remember. It pounded the roof and rushed out the downspouts with maniacal force. The rain felt like a beast trying to batter its way into their home.

He opened the freezer door and pressed his forehead into the packed frost and clenched his jaw and couldn't bring himself to leave the small frozen space.

"Whatcha doin', Joseph?"

"And what happen if *I* die first?"

"Not gonna happen unless you kill yourself."

"Maybe I kill myself."

"If you kill yourself Rosie'll come and get me."

He ran back and stood before Clara. Had she lost her mind?

"Rosie? You a very funny woman, Clara. You think Rosie rich husband gonna care? You think he gonna take you in his big fancy house if I die? When last time Rosie come see you?"

"I pray for them every day, Joseph."

"Yah, very good. You pray, pray, pray."

"People change. When push comes to shove—"

"When push come to shove? You mean when Rosie put gun to Gordon head? Why our daughter marry this kind of man? I tell you why—"

"Stop it, Joseph. It don't matter. I'm the one dying, not you."

"Why you talk crazy?"

"I'm not crazy."

"You sound like a crazy woman."

"Dear Jesus, look at me."

"Yah, I see you. I see Clara."

"No, you see Lucy."

"Oh, so now you compare yourself to stupid bird?"

"Poor Ricardo."

"What da hell dat mean, poor Ricardo?"

"Poor Ricardo, poor Ricardo, poor Ricardo."

"What da hell you saying, Clara?"

"I'm saying what you say all the time."

"Okay, okay, yah, poor Ricardo. I wrong to feel bad for Ricardo?"

"Poor Joseph."

"What da hell, Clara. What you wan from me?"

On impulse, Clara reached for the left wheel to jerk away from her husband, but reconsidered.

She put her hand on her lap over the rosary beads. She looked all around, as if she were in a place she had never been before. She looked everywhere but at Joseph. She scratched the top of her head and started working the beads, one by one, praying with her fingers rather than her lips.

"What's da matter with you, Clara? You think I wan you die?"

"If things were different. If *you* were in this wheelchair, I don't know if I..."

She looked up at him and whispered, "I don't know how you do it, Joseph."

"You do same for me, Clara," he said and walked away from her to watch the downpour through the window. Clara turned the wheelchair so she could see him.

"Yesterday, after you left for the supermarket, I prayed God to take me. I wanted Him to take me before you got home."

She waited, watched Joseph shake his head. She cleared her throat.

"Shit, Joseph. You know what He said to me? So what happens to Joseph if you die today, huh?"

"Aghhh!" Joseph shouted, swinging his arms in exasperation. The thought of Clara dead and him free to be with Nora had filled his mouth with a sweet taste for just one terrible instant.

He walked to the kitchen sink, spit out the thought and rubbed his teeth and gums hard with cold water. He closed his eyes and prayed that Clara would lack the power to read his thoughts.

"Come here," she said.

"What, Clara, what? You pray. So God no like your prayer. So what? Fine. What you wan from me?"

"I want you to go to Mass."

"Mass? What you mean? I have Mass here with you every Sunday."

"The lady from church don't say Mass."

"She bring Eucharist. She pray with us, no? She pray good."

"I want you to go to Mass at Immaculate Heart tomorrow."

"Oh yah? An who get door if I no here when lady come?"

"She don't get here 'til twelve. You can go to the ten o'clock."

Joseph shook his head, checked his watch, walked up and down the room shaking his head some more. Finally, he stopped in front of Clara and said, "God say dis?"

Clara looked up and stared at him, as though she could not understand what he was asking.

"Clara, God say you make Joseph go to church? Tell truth."

"Yeah, Joseph, I think so."

Joseph sighed. "Okay, I go to ten o'clock Mass before lady come."

THE TEA-COLORED LAKE slept beneath morning sunlight that moved over the waters like sparkling fingers.

Joseph tread carefully over the muddy bank near the bridge until he found a small clearing in a thicket of reeds—what he considered might be Ricardo and Lucy's nest—but there were no swans there.

The damp morning air pressed the lake's surface smooth, the way Clara's thumb pressed her rosary crucifix. Joseph felt nostalgic as he gazed across the lake to where the little ranch house would be, somewhere behind those waterfront houses.

"You rub dat thing so much make Jesus's face disappear," he once said to her a long time ago.

A long time ago she had replied, "His face don't disappear, Joseph, cause I see it when I look at yours."

It had been one of their few good days over the last several years, and all he could do when she said that was wave her off with a laugh.

There was time to kill before Mass, so he worked his way back across the slippery bank toward the bridge and wondered if Lucy had been assumed into swan heaven.

"Where are you, Ricardo?" he called out, and tried to imagine a scenario in which Ricardo would take his own life, but thought it unlikely given that he was a swan.

"Where are you, Ricardo?" he called out again and remained for a while, serenaded by the morning's silence.

Ricardo's predicament and Lucy's demise occupied Joseph's thoughts as he drove to church. He envisioned Ricardo in some other lake floating with princely distinction beside a plump female that he would be eager to impregnate.

The prospect gave Joseph comfort. The Jesus figurine attached to the top of the old Buick's dashboard was always smiling, always stretching out its tiny palms in a gesture of acceptance. The plastic rosary that hung from the rearview mirror swung to and fro, measuring out a promising new timeline. God was pleased that Ricardo had rejected despair and chosen happiness after all, Joseph decided.

It was unusually warm, so like springtime. He looked at his arms and realized he was wearing a short-sleeved shirt with no jacket. He rolled down the driver side window feeling a little lightheaded as he drove, a tad disconnected from the streets and the houses and the surprising trees that were filled with leaves.

But how did this happen? Had winter come and gone? What madness! To think such a thing. Better to think of Friday. Friday would come in five days. He would return to the supermarket. He would see Nora again.

He and Nora would have had a few days to put the *Meats* woman in perspective. All was not lost. They would learn from the bad experience. He would be more careful. He would say to her, "Do you like coffee?" In the designated refreshments area of the super-market, they could sit and have coffee. A cup of coffee, that is all. The coffee there was good and would only cost one dollar for two cups, with as much creamer and sugar as a soul could want at no extra cost.

They would exchange a word or two about the sudden change in the weather, the uptick in food prices, what a good idea the refreshments area was, and so on.

Maybe they would share how long each had lived in the area and where they had lived before. Maybe he would compliment Nora on her boots. Maybe. He would have to see...

It had been a long time since he had driven into the parking lot at Immaculate Heart. He was too early, but he wanted to secure a seat in the back, on the left, so he could leave right after communion before the priest processed out the middle aisle.

He got out of the Buick after warding off the temptation to drive away and took a few steps toward the church. He stooped to pick up a quarter off the asphalt. A good omen. The two cups of coffee would now cost him only seventy-five cents.

He fingered the change in his pocket and saw a car pull up near the front entrance of the church and park in a space reserved for the disabled. Joseph froze. It could be anyone's car, and the woman getting out through the driver side could be a woman like Nora, very similar to Nora, but not her...

Joseph blinked hard to better see a woman that was and was not Nora. Regardless of who she was, she must not see him. He limped back to his car—an old hip flexor strain suddenly roused—and pretended to search the ground while keeping one eye on the woman.

The woman's arms disappeared and her shoulders jerked as she withdrew a wheelchair from the trunk of her car. She pried it open with the fatigued precision of someone who has performed the act thousands of times.

Joseph straightened his back and watched the woman fold herself into the front passenger side and extract a broken man wearing a suit and tie, and maneuver him with her well-trained hands and bent back onto the wheelchair.

He told himself it was not Nora. How could it be? He told himself the man was her father, not her husband. He got back in the Buick and watched Nora roll her husband in his wheelchair into the church fifteen minutes before ten o'clock Mass.

Joseph sat in his car. He needed to calm down and think this through. If God had instructed Clara to tell him to go to this Mass, it must be because God intended for him to see Nora with her husband, who was confined to a wheelchair. If that were so, it must be for one of two reasons: for him, Joseph, to serve as a consolation to Nora, or for him to never see her again.

They were easy to spot as there were two front pews in the wings of the church reserved for the disabled. He decided to seat himself behind and at an angle that made it easy for him to observe them without himself being observed.

Joseph rose with the congregation and sat and rose and prayed and knelt and prayed and rose and prayed and did it all in a droning blur, prompted and moved and impelled by the *Mystical Body*, or the ordinary bodies, or muscle memory, or spirit memory from a time when there were no wheelchairs in his life.

He gazed at the priest, the deacon, the lector, the cantor and the altar servers as though he were watching them on TV. But Nora looked real, as did the man in the wheelchair who increasingly looked like Clara. He rubbed his eyes and tried to shake away the sharpening image, but no matter how much he tilted his head or raised it or lowered it or drew it back or pushed it forward, he could not halt the broken man's metamorphosis into his poor Clara, his Clara who was held together by steel, rubber, vinyl and duct tape.

He stood up with the entire congregation after the *Prayer of Consecration* but stepped out of the pew and walked to the back of the church and through the glass doors into the narthex on his way out to the parking lot.

"Joseph!"

He flinched, expecting to be swatted down by the Almighty's hand.

"Joseph."

He recognized the man from the village community center. He'd played dominos with him once or twice. He remembered him as a friendly man, quick to smile, but he was not smiling as he walked up to him.

"Joseph," he said. "Ned Pento. You remember me?"

"Yah, Ned."

"Long time no see. How are you?"

"Good, Ned. How you?"

"Gettin' by… I'm an usher now. Signed up about a month ago."

"Oh, yah? Good, good."

Ned looked concerned. "No Communion today?"

"Oh, yah. No, no receive today."

Ned grimaced and pressed his hands together in what seemed to Joseph a gesture of supplication.

"There's a group here, Joseph. We meet Tuesday nights at seven in the chapel."

Joseph stared at the man, puzzled.

"It's coming on two years for me."

"Two years?"

"Two years, Joseph."

"Ah."

"When I heard your wife's name during the announcements for today's Mass intentions—six months already, hard to believe—it made me think back to my Emily... Look, Joseph, if there's anything I can do."

"Yah, okay, Ned."

Joseph rushed out of the church and drove back home. He turned the key to the front door slowly, paying particular attention to the smooth oily clunk of the dead bolt as it slid open. He stepped inside and closed the door with extreme care as though afraid he would wake someone.

The TV was tuned to the Catholic station and set on Mute. He watched the priest behind the altar wipe the chalice dry with a white cloth and then watched him fold and place the cloth over the chalice and the paten atop the chalice and another folded white cloth over the paten and hand the liturgical vessels to the deacon who carried them away. Joseph took the remote control and turned the volume on low.

The priest said the final prayer and made the sign of the cross over the congregation and television audience. Joseph whispered the words of dismissal along with the deacon, *The Mass is ended, go in peace*, and the congregation responded, *Thanks be to God*.

He turned his head and looked at the empty wheelchair and then walked to the birdcage. He stuck his forefinger through the bars, and Randy pecked at it with little enthusiasm, as if solely to oblige the old man. Joseph talked to Randy about the lake and the swans and Nora and the man in the wheelchair and Ned Pento.

Then he took a clean cloth and wiped the thin layer of dust from Clara's unfinished puzzle. He stared at Rex Harrison and at Audrey Hepburn's broken face, and he held up the piece with Audrey's missing eye. Unable to bring himself to finish what Clara had started, he put that piece back on the table where Clara had always preferred to keep it.

Joseph worked from the borders in, carefully separating the attached pieces one at a time. He placed the pieces one by one in the colorful cardboard box that depicted Audrey and Rex at the horse track. Audrey in her fine dress with parasol and voluminous hat, and suave Rex, the two of them held together by the subtle grip of a new conception.

He left Audrey's incomplete face for last. He stared a long time at the pretty eye that had studied Clara's face for weeks. He studied Audrey's eye from various angles and heights, as though the eye (or the one set aside) might reveal to him something he had failed to consider. But he tired of this and completed his task, putting every last piece into the box. He taped the box shut and placed it on a shelf in the tiny enclosed front porch.

Then Joseph folded the wheelchair and leaned it against the wall in the porch. He thought it best to take the wheelchair and the puzzle to the village community center, where a small room was set aside for donated goods. He would do that tomorrow morning after breakfast.

Then he would come home and make a list of other things to give away, lots of them. But Randy he would keep, and he would keep the rosary with the crucifix rubbed smooth by Clara's good fingers.

All About Wendy

WENDY LIKES TO STRIP-DANCE before her dresser mirror. I admit to enjoying the view, but I know her performance is always, like everything else, all about Wendy. Not for a moment do I think she can hold a candle to Bernadette, but I left Bernadette for Wendy anyway.

Not because Bernadette is a career secretary, nor because she's older and a divorced mom. She's entirely unlike any woman I've ever met, and I mean that in a good way.

The thing is, she got inside me. To be honest, at this point in my life I don't want things to get complicated. I'm still a young man. I like having options. I prefer simplicity. I don't need or want a complicated relationship.

It wasn't easy. I dropped her off at her apartment. I told her I was doing us both a favor. She seemed numbed by my words. Didn't say anything, didn't cry, beg, or guilt me into changing my mind. Bernadette is a lovely woman.

PLENTY OF GUYS can make a case for Wendy. Aside from her carnal gifts and up-tempo sexuality, she's a math wiz and topnotch budget analyst. She prizes numbers and the bottom line more than she prizes persons, animals, trees, or the most heartfelt song.

This is not necessarily a bad thing. To Wendy, a person's life is defined by financial net worth.

In Wendy's world love and commitment fall within that family of old-fashioned ideas that are always in demand, like the bestselling products of world dominator companies like Proctor and Gamble and Coca Cola. Love and commitment and other fuzzy feeling concepts exist to be plotted, quantified and monetized by *Smart* people.

That is what Wendy believes. You can see why that kind of woman might appeal to a certain kind of man.

Wendy's persona and existential valuations make it easy for me to dismiss the possibility she might possess any emotional history of consequence or harbor desires of the heart. I see her absence of sentiment as wonderfully convenient, and in good faith, I have come to expect from her a commitment to reciprocal indifference.

SOMETHING HAS HAPPENED. Saturday night we were lying in bed recovering from a good solid romp, when Wendy starts to rattle off names beginning with *W*: William, Wyclef, Walker, Whitney, Wanda, Wilfreda, and so on.

"What are you doing?" I ask.

"Playing a list game, listing names that could work—let's say just for argument's sake—if you and I were to produce offspring."

Ho! Am I reading too much into these words?

I let it go, but Tuesday rolls around and Wendy wants to know why I cancelled dinner at her place on Wednesday. This is new. We never question each other's change of plans, so this deviation gets my attention in a big way.

Her expression remains all business, however, suggesting this is a question of professional courtesy more than anything else. Gazing at her, I feel as though I am holding one of those annoying pieces of unsolicited mail with *The Courtesy of a Reply is Requested* embossed in gold calligraphy on the front of the envelope.

I can see what she is up to. I refuse, on principle, to extend the courtesy of a response. I stare at her, and when I see her mask begin to disintegrate, my suspicion appears to be confirmed. Her left brow twitches, her lips part. It is as if she has decided to say something she should not, but then decides not to, but then does.

"Please don't tell me you're seeing that homely Bernadette woman again."

She follows up with a laugh as abrupt and ugly as a belch. No, I haven't been with Bernadette, who is not homely at all, nor have I mentioned her name in months, but I refuse to dignify Wendy's remark with a response.

Wendy won't allow my silence to wield power and quickly changes the subject. She mentions a glitch in the new Information Assurance training video everyone on Post is required to view.

"Who puts these things together anyway, and how much is it costing the taxpayer?" she asks rhetorically.

WHATEVER RESERVATIONS I have been harboring about putting an end to my arrangement with Wendy are dispelled once and for all during our last evening together. Wendy looks me in the eye and says, "A beautiful woman is like a retirement plan. The more you put into her today, the more you get back tomorrow."

A retirement plan?

"You see, one big bad decision can utterly derail a life. It could be getting sucked into a Ponzi scheme, failing to read the fine print on a contract, joining the wrong crowd, etcetera. On the flip side, one big, really good decision can guarantee lifelong success and satisfaction. An example would be forming a partnership with the right person.

Who do you choose to be your partner? Who makes your success inevitable?

"I'm convinced, for example, that you and I would make a great team. We could make lots of money together. Aren't you tired of working for the Government? Aren't you tired of redundancy and waste? And my God, aren't you sick and tired of having a ceiling on how much money you can make?"

A business partnership? Is that what this is about? Or is Wendy in the midst of discovering metaphor?

She talks at length about money and why you can never have enough. She shares with me an impressive understanding of options and futures and offshore tax havens like the Cayman Islands and Singapore where she suggests buying vacation condos to rent and opening bank accounts.

She makes a passing reference to a substantial inheritance coming her way any day now and further entices me with the idea of answering to no one. Then she renders in startling detail the creation of a market-dominating wedding favors home business.

"I've done the supply and demand research, scrutinized the competition, generated projections, identified suitable suppliers, completed all the legwork, essentially. I did secure an EIN, if you're wondering, and set up a merchant account to receive payments. The website is up and running and traffic is starting to trickle in. Still looking into ways of bolstering SEO; that's ongoing, of course. Come here, let me show you."

I hesitate, then follow her into her bedroom, having months ago been programmed to do so. She sits in front of her laptop stroking keys at the speed of light.

"Here's the Home Page," she says.

Neat groupings of little bottles and hearts and pouches with pink, red, and pale-yellow ribbons and laces appear almost three-dimensional. They cry out to me, *Touch me! Touch me! Touch me!* When I say nothing, she gets up from her chair.

"Why do you keep shaking your head like that?" she says.

Even as I am muttering "No, no, no," Wendy's strangely contorting face seems on the verge of bursting into tears, but not a tear spills, nor the faintest whimper escapes her lips. I watch her features twist and churn into a battlefield where multiple women grapple for dominance: Wendy the Baffled, Wendy the Outraged, Wendy the Wounded, Wendy the Cruel, and so on.

There is no way I can have prepared for all of them. Even as the words "What could you possibly have been thinking?" are tumbling out of my mouth, I know I have blundered badly. I watch Wendy's hand rise up as though hailing a taxi, her ice blue eyes not quite set on me as on a place through and beyond me. She slaps my face so hard I can hear my skin buzz. I lose count of how many times she screams the peculiar command, "Get out of me!" She shoves me toward the wall and pounds my head with her soft round fists.

After the initial shock of her assault, I find myself engrossed by what is happening. Her rage pleases me, I realize, and her harmless blows feel uniquely gratifying. As I grab and hold her flailing arms, I imagine—in a blur of greedy animal optimism—that I have detected a kind of collusion between us suggested by the languid surging of her body, the accented sway of her full hips.

But it is a moment of weakness on my part, one quickly dispatched by the sorry spectacle I am witnessing in that all too familiar dresser mirror.

"Stop!" I shout. "Stop it right now!"

One shout for her, one for me.

Finally, sensing her resentful compliance, if not surrender, I release her and stare a few moments at her flushed face.

"I thought we had an understanding," I say and turn to leave, but she is right behind me, the point of her shoe clipping the heel of mine.

"An understanding?" she shouts rising on the balls of her feet as I am thumbing my dislodged shoe back into place.

"What I don't understand," she says wild-eyed, "is how you managed to get inside me. Because, truth be told, you're nothing but a self-centered shit!"

Such rich irony. I am not inclined to argue the point, however. I decide to let her have the last word. It is the least I can do.

Wendy giggles when I open the front door. I turn around more confused by my impulse to indulge her than by her increasingly erratic behavior. Like Superwoman, she tears open her blouse, and I watch the little white buttons pop, fly, and bounce off the plush burgundy carpet. I follow the arc of her bra as it sails across the living room. It is an uncharacteristically dramatic gesture on her part, and the sight of her glistening breasts heaps another layer of confusion upon the occasion.

She begins to jiggle all over with unbridled laughter. I close the door to seal off potential prying by local busybodies. I search for meaning, but our eyes are like the repelling poles of two like-aligned magnets. I gaze at the dark hole of her gaping mouth and puzzle over the tear that rolls down her cheek.

Then abruptly she stops laughing. She looks deep into my eyes. *Beseechingly* is the word that comes to mind. She nearly wins me over. I begin to preview how this might unfold and admit to feeling a pleasant tingling in my loins. But I come to my senses, brush aside temptation and walk out the door.

On the street I ponder Wendy's many masks, her complex and conflicted nature. What is it she really wants, I ask myself? Who can say? There's a lot going on in that handsome head of hers...

You know what, Doc? I should give her a call, see how she's managing. Bernadette, that is. I meant Bernadette, of course...

Uhm, Doctor Bannon? Why are you staring at me like that?

The Battlefield

DARREN DIDN'T CALL.

Instead, he had his perky, young intern leave Bonniah a message to let her know he had been called to an impromptu meeting of the partners, and would not be able to drive her to the airport, as he had planned. A limo would pick her up at home to take her, and he would call her later tonight.

The ride to the airport was pure misery. He would not call, she knew, but in Darren's world, appearances mattered, and given the intern's involvement, it was the right thing to say. The weather did not help, as rain began to pelt the limo, eliciting the standard observation from the driver, who looked like an undertaker but for the tattooed hand.

"Yes," she agreed, "the weather has been awful."

They left it at that.

Darren's response to displeasure, she had discovered early on, was to inflict pain by tiny cuts. The slow bleed was a recurring theme in their marriage, and Bonniah wondered daily now if she would have enough blood left tomorrow to continue to be the wife he had secured for himself thirty years ago.

At the airport the limo driver placed her bag on the terminal curb. She handed him an extra twenty to supplement the standard fifteen percent gratuity automatically apportioned by her husband's account, and they exchanged awkward *thank-yous*.

She checked in, passed through security, located her departure gate, and boarded the plane without incident, moving along on autopilot. Upon settling herself in her window seat the specifics of how she had gotten from the limo drop-off point to her window seat eluded her. It was all a blur.

But she did remember the faded tattoo of a heart encircled by thorny stems on the top of the limo driver's right hand as he set her bag on the terminal curb. The tattooed hand had been there the entire drive to the airport, perched on the steering wheel like a colorful frog, and she had thought to ask him about it, but the prospect of entering into involved conversation with a retired factory worker (or janitor or stock clerk or delivery man or whatever type of work such men might secure for themselves) had the dank disquieting feel of descending to a catacomb.

Instead, she had pretended to read one of the magazines slipped into the sleeve of the seatback in front of her, so as to hide her thoughts from the driver. She did not want him thinking inappropriate things. That is, she did not want him getting the wrong idea, especially with Darren so near. Darren was always nearby and there was nothing she could do about that.

Of late, especially, she had often recalled the moment thirty-one years ago when the solemn, remote valedictorian approached her after the graduates and their families had begun to disperse. Perhaps emboldened by the flawless (if a bit stiff) delivery of his thoughtful (if somewhat unoriginal) speech, he had waded far beyond his comfort zone to come to her, offering, in a faltering voice, "I wish to say something to you, Bonniah, if you would permit me. I wish to say that I have never met anyone quite like you."

His moment of weakness had stunned her. She had had suspicions of his vulnerability, of course, perhaps having been the only one on campus interested enough to pay close attention. Darren Ackerley was something of an anachronism. He wore his old-fashioned decorum like a tweed jacket every single day, and to his classmates he projected vaguely as a thing or an idea rather than as a person. He was like an oxidized bronze statue receding on the edge of one's vision.

He avoided humans, in general, and Kirk his roommate in particular, along with all the other *fatuous philosophizers*, as he called them, with their *wobble-headed all-night ramblings*, drained beer kegs and sticky floors suggestive of *dispiriting promiscuities...*

The sudden breach in his person superseded anything Bonniah could have anticipated. How could he not have known she would recognize the fear in his voice, this young man who had worked so hard to project and preserve an image of self-assured exclusivity?

She had felt a flush of embarrassment at having witnessed his debility but was secretly flattered. She smiled to reassure him as well as herself, and on an impulse took his hand in both of hers. Her touch caused him to wince for an instant, as though his metal exterior had transformed just then into delicate flesh.

He did manage a nervous smile and she was encouraged by it. His need of her made her feel special, and she confused that need for love. Later, after the years had swept away all illusion, she would often wonder if the unsolicited knowledge she acquired the day she peered inside him had smothered love's beginnings before it could breathe itself into self-giving.

But the young live on a separate plane of existence. Hadn't his need come to be enough for her? And wasn't love just another luxury, a notion subject to the amusement of television audiences and the sentimentality of fools? Wouldn't his need of her have to suffice at this point in her life? His need of the smart, gentle-eyed girl no one was like, the one who, ironically, no longer existed?

So many questions. What to think? Had Darren foreseen her lack of ambition? Would things have been different had she put her mind and talents to better use once the children were gone? Did being president of the Fire Department Ladies Auxiliary and having her name listed on the Sponsor's page in the Library's Annual Report count for anything?

She pressed the fingers of her right hand between her eyebrows and began to rub gently in a circular motion. She was tired, and the time she would have to be away from him, though only an extended weekend, increasingly bore the weight of odyssey.

It was not too late to get up. Not too late to walk down the aisle and out the plane and go home. It would please him, she knew, though he would not admit it. If she decided for him, right now, would her decision herald the beginning of something new between them? A transition to something different and better?

But Bonniah existed in parts, each possessed to some degree by its own will. Her hand, for example, had its own mind and wandered from her lap. She felt it move inside her bag, fondling the printout of Sarah's email. The other hand worked with it in tandem to unfold the stapled sheets and to place them on her lap face down so that four blank white rectangles stared up at her. A finger took it upon itself to trace the vertical seam, then the horizontal, top to bottom, left to right.

Her sister had always led an unorthodox life. One day toward the end of dinner, soon after Sarah's first divorce, Bonniah had casually mentioned to Darren that Sarah had moved to Spain. She would do that now and then, administer Sarah to him in small doses in the hope of inoculating him against whatever he detested in her.

Sarah was working as an English-speaking guide at the *Alcázar* and at the great cathedral in Seville, she told him. She elaborated further, citing the large number of English-speaking tourists who visited the capital of Andalucía year-round. Darren's silence was expected—so not exceedingly disappointing—but as she stood up holding her plate and glass, Darren said, in what sounded to her a surprisingly congenial tone, "Sarah defines disordered."

Was that a smile? She couldn't be sure, but the words echoed of promise in the dull quiet dining room like the preamble to a long-anticipated pronouncement. It wasn't so much *what* he said but that it *was* said, and without rancor, her sister's name tossed into the gray mix of their lives like a splash of sound and color. But as too often occurred with Bonniah, hunger for reconciliation and harmony blinded her to reality.

"It's funny you say that," she said, "given the latest—" but his gaze hacked her words short.

Several choices had presented themselves to her in that instant, various arrangements of words she might speak and facial gestures and body language she might project, but she froze. In that frozen state she wondered if she, an intelligent, well-educated woman, shouldn't have known there was to be no repartee regarding Sarah.

There he was, studying her. She had tried to buffer herself from his scrutiny. But there came that sinking feeling again, the nauseating suspicion that he was performing something akin to numerical calculations and was finding his margin of gain to have suffered yet another incremental loss as the result of one more unwanted dose of Sarah.

Even as she continued to sink into a familiar state of misery, Bonniah witnessed her husband's own descent.

How devastating to acknowledge finally that she was the source of *his* unhappiness. He had smiled, perhaps embarrassed by their shared knowledge of her new self-assessment, and excused himself. There was work waiting for him in the study. Work was always waiting for Darren.

The sheets trembled beneath her hand. The hidden words bumped up against the four white rectangles, agitating to be read. Or so it seemed. Could it be the runway vibrating? She folded the sheets and placed them back in her bag.

Sarah would understand. No one Bonniah had ever met suffered slights and disappointments more admirably than her free-spirited sister. After all of her disasters, Sarah remained the stronger of the two. Sarah would shake off whatever it was that had led her to write that strange note, and Bonniah's decision to backtrack and not go to Seattle would prove to be the best thing for Sarah, and for Darren, and consequently for herself as well.

Upon seeing Bonniah, and confirming the choice she had made, Darren's silence would be dignified rather than triumphant or condescending. His expression would be like that of a person in the midst of unraveling an overly involved thought. He would not comment on her change of plans, but he would be secretly pleased, satisfied in that deep place that was off limits, but that perhaps now he might begin to open to her.

Having savored the favorable development a while, he would ask if she wanted a drink. She would say yes, and he would prepare her a martini and himself a scotch, and then he would stand by the big bay window and stare out into the darkness of night, one hand inside his trousers pocket, the other holding his glass straight down against his leg, jiggling the ice every minute or so before raising the glass to his lips. And she would sit and watch him and the darkness of night through the window and wonder if that would be enough for them.

Even as the metallic snap of the released seat belt buckle echoed in Bonniah's ear, a large, brown, intricate bulk of a woman appeared to her left, filling all space and limiting Bonniah's options in an uncompromising manner. After a series of loud, irregular thump-slam-thump maneuvers, the woman plopped herself into the empty aisle seat next to her, challenging the limits of the seat's structural integrity.

Only after properly distributing her prodigious frame did she turn to acknowledge Bonniah. Her smile was broad and disarming and made Bonniah think of big fresh strawberries and milk and a bright sunny kitchen, and of Sarah.

Still smiling, but with a certain melancholy now, as though smiling at the memory of her smile, the woman rolled forward, bending her mass to pluck a hardcover book out of her bag. She set the book on her lap with ritualistic care, took a deep shuddering breath, and plunged into its world of words.

Amazing how the unplanned movement of lips and mouth could change everything! Some smiles anointed time and space, gave comfort, altered perspective, swept away layers of confusion. This unexpected smile had transported Sarah across the American continent, transformed her sister into a wonderfully rich buoyant form that warmed Bonniah's heart and kept her securely seated.

She looked out the window. Rain was splashing off service vehicles and luggage carts and airplanes. She had never been one to be completely taken in by signs and wonders, but she could not deny the sudden longing she felt for her sister.

Her decision to continue on to Seattle had as much to do with her marriage as it had to do with Sarah. Things could not remain as they were, she decided. She was tired of the long silent battles. Her blood pressure was too high. And Darren? There was a history of cancer on his side of the family. The plane began to groan and she withstood a brief passing shudder.

She steadied her head against the seat back.

Darren, are you with someone?

During one of their silent pyrrhic campaigns, Bonniah had gone to the movies. She had read a review of Almodóvar's *Women on the Verge of A Nervous Breakdown* and had been intrigued.

She had imagined Sarah sitting next to her in the near-empty theater, their heads close together, the two sisters laughing at the same funny parts. Whenever it got too quiet Sarah would touch her sister's hand and whisper, "Think hard about the kind of woman you want to be, Bonnie."

Walking out of the theater entertaining thoughts of self-fulfillment, Bonniah had immediately been challenged by the persistent awareness of how easily a woman in a man's world could succumb to hopelessness. She vowed it would not happen to her, but as she approached her front door she wondered if she, Bonniah Ackerley, could ever find the way to become the strong courageous woman she seemed always to be pursuing.

The flight to London after their son's wedding had teased her with a new way of seeing and understanding. She had woken from fitful sleep to spy a narrow arc of melon sun hanging in a milky vastness. The sun and John's smile upon seeing his bride marching up the aisle on her father's arm had become joined to one another, leaving no separation between then and now.

In that moment of joyful awareness, time meant nothing. The moment was pure gift. The universe was smiling at her. Or was it God that was smiling?

"Love rising like the sun," she had heard herself say.

How wonderfully palpable had been that warm bright floating feeling. She could almost taste its sweetness, feel it drip down her chin. She had smiled and tapped the window thanking whatever or whomever had touched her so perfectly and, on an impulse, had turned to her husband.

Under normal circumstances she would never interrupt his reading, but there was something far greater than their burdensome marital history at work, and she knew—as well as she knew anything—that such lightness of being was meant to be shared. She touched her husband's forearm and informed him that she always chose the window seat because she wanted to see angels. Darren pondered what she had said for a few moments wearing his look of ebbing tolerance and without a word went right back to reading his *Smithsonian*.

Had he caught a glimpse of Sarah in his wife's rare attempt at frivolity?

Two years gone, and here she was again, looking for angels. She redirected the overhead vent away from her head and tried to remember when she had last eaten or had something to drink. Her mouth was dry. The wind had shifted and now the hard-splashing raindrops streamed fast down her window.

She should have left when she had the chance. Her sister's propensity for melodrama could be maddening. Sarah would have found a way to move forward without her, as she always did. Was Sarah being manipulative, as Darren had suggested?

Darren? Are you with her?

No matter how much she had tried to downplay it, the sudden appearance of Lena Sparks in their lives had unsettled Bonniah. The girl's uncanny grasp of her husband's peculiarities in so brief a period was troubling and bordered on covetous. It was difficult for Bonniah to sound natural when she spoke to her husband's intern or spoke about her to Darren.

There was something disturbing about the way the girl moved. Suggestive. No, obscene, actually. Bonniah wondered if others also pondered Lena Spark's musky scent, and like her, imagined unsavory scenarios.

Until Lena, the idea of Darren with another woman had seemed comical to her. Before she met Darren, she had had two lovers, both of whom were far more enthusiastic about her womanly charms than Darren.

He never did have much of a sex drive, though she felt that in his prime, with a slight adjustment of attitude, he might have gotten some consideration for the sexy lead in any number of television legal or medical dramas.

Darren was driven by another love. On his fiftieth birthday he began preparing in their attic the foundation for an enormous diorama of the Battle of Gettysburg.

It was nearly inconceivable to Bonniah that a man who enjoyed erecting miniature silos more than his manhood would invest precious time and energy initiating and sustaining an adulterous affair. Even so...

One evening, prompted by loneliness, Bonniah had climbed the stairs to the attic waving her second martini before her like a lantern. Darren was utterly absorbed with his project and paid her no attention.

She had known for some time that the foundation he had laid for their marriage would never be quite as sound or lovingly nurtured as the one he had laid for his spectacular battlefield. She understood the diorama held for Darren a complexity and beauty she had once possessed but no longer.

So why was she there? To wage combat?

"This is Barlow's Knoll," he had said as she was turning to leave. "And these are the guns of Battery G, 4th U.S. Artillery."

She had raised her glass in mock salute to the tiny forms and figures, spilling her drink onto the planked floor. She laughed at her clumsiness and at him. What do you say to someone who flaunts his infidelity, who tries to woo you into it? What can you do but laugh or scream?

Walking down the stairs from the attic exercising the laxity of movement furnished by two strong drinks, Bonniah stopped halfway to listen to herself: *If he bleeds you until there's nothing left, will he still need you?*

The following morning her coffee had tasted bitter. She had failed him. How rare the invitation to enter into his one passion. An opportunity squandered. Marriage should not be this hard, and Sarah should have contacted her earlier, given her more time to prepare her husband.

"We've exhausted this topic," he had said, barely glancing at her. "I'll be back later to drive you to the airport."

Instead, he had instructed Lena Sparks to leave a message. What was one more little cut anyway?

Bonniah took her sister's note out of her bag and began to read:

Bonnie,

Remember how we would read each other's diaries when we were kids? You wanted me to understand you. You were afraid things wouldn't come out right if you said them, so you wrote them down for me to read.

Now I'm doing the same because I want you to know things I don't think would come out right if I said them.

I've been trying to understand the big picture in light of the past few months, which I describe below. Wasn't sure till now that I wanted you to read this. Anyway, here goes...

◊

The men laughed at something Billings said. The usual, a snide reference to a client's failure to grasp a concept, or maybe it was a comment about someone's attire.

I wasn't paying much attention. I was doodling, thinking about the time we drew the Von Trapp kids after seeing The Sound of Music with Mom and Dad. I was trying to draw Maria singing and whirling on the mountaintop, her arms outstretched, so free and happy...

Billings asked me a question. I started to cough, pretending my coffee had gone down the wrong way. I got up, waved off everybody's concern and walked out of the meeting and out of the building.

After a while I saw a little girl standing alone on the sidewalk. She could not have been more than five years old. People were walking by as if she wasn't there. She was staring at me with big, round eyes and wearing an ill-fitting green jacket. The damp, chilly April breeze made her wavy hair bob on her shoulders. Her lower lip began to quiver as she looked up and down the street. As I walked toward her she started crying in breathless little grunts. I said, "Don't cry, darling. I'll help you find your mommy."

I reached to touch the little girl's cheek when a shabbily dressed woman appeared and snatched her away.

I felt compelled to follow them. I almost lost them in the late morning crowd after I stumbled into a man when my heel came down on something small and hard. The man caught me and looked at me in confusion as though he could not understand how someone so well dressed could be so clumsy.

I saw the woman and her little girl, and as I drew close the woman came to a stop and turned to face me, swinging the child behind her. "What do you want?" she said in an angry Slavic voice.

I was embarrassed because I didn't know how to answer her. "What do I want?" That was what came out of my mouth. I hadn't asked myself that question in a very long time. Not since I made the decision to divorce Ted.

I must have looked like a lunatic to that woman. "What do I want?" I repeated. "I don't know. Nothing, only to tell you that your daughter is lovely."

How pathetic, Bonnie. Unhappy aging woman chases after younger woman's child. My goodness, have you ever heard of such a thing?

The woman appeared confused for a moment. Then it all seemed to make sense to her. She looked me over, top to bottom, like the man I had collided with. She took her time looking me over and then smiled as if she possessed damning evidence against me.

I wanted her to understand I was not the person I appeared to be. She shook her head in disgust, turned around and marched off, tugging at the child's arm to make her keep up.

The cool breeze sent a chill through my body. My ankle hurt, but I buttoned my jacket and walked on. The thought of going back to the office filled me with disgust.

I continued to walk and walk for a long time, leaving the business district behind. I went into places I'd never have imagined trespassing, shabby, dreary places where the invisible poor live out their lives. I realized that a prosperous-looking white woman in this part of town was asking for trouble, but I was beyond caring.

I reached down to my ankle, pressed my fingers against the swelling. I needed a place to sit. I came upon an old brownstone church with statues of a man and woman recessed into the facade on either side of the entrance. Mary and Joseph, as it turned out, their clear alabaster faces serene, if somewhat remote. But remote suited me, and I needed a little serenity too.

I could sit inside, rest, get warm. It would be quiet and peaceful. I would think things through, figure out what to do next. I can assure you the irony that I had ended up in front of a church instead of a crack house was not lost on me.

I began to climb the steps, but stopped when I felt a sharp pain in my ankle. The church doors swung open just then and several people spilled out onto the landing and came down the steps. I felt uncomfortable standing there. It was obvious I didn't belong. I turned and gazed down the street, pretending to be waiting for a ride.

When they had all left, I resumed my climb up the stone steps. One last person appeared. He looked like a giant. He frightened me but he was just a harmless old man with an ugly scar on his forehead. He saw my fear and his expression softened. He invited me into the church and left me there, sitting on a pew. I stared at the bloodied Christ on the cross behind the altar, so beautiful in a horrific way. But I felt safe there, as safe as I've felt since we were kids, Bonnie. Since before the accident.

I didn't go back to work. I didn't care to. I didn't want to listen to Billings anymore. Every day at the same time I would go back to that brownstone church. The giant always greeted me and then would disappear. I would sit for a while, feeling safe, remembering the good times you and I had when we were kids.

One day I asked the giant to sit with me. He nodded, as if it were his duty. I got to know him very well. He was the sexton at the church, he explained, the one who did all the maintenance.

Tanek Oleski and I got married in that church a couple of months later. Tanek was the kindest person I have ever known.

◊

Since Mom and Dad died, we've both had a hard time of it, haven't we, Bonnie?

Now things have changed again and I have to see you as soon as you can get away. I know with Darren it's not so easy...

Maybe you would have preferred I'd kept this all to myself. But you're my sister, and I don't know who else I can turn to.

Sarah

BONNIAH PLACED SARAH'S NOTE on the table and stared at the stapled sheets warming beneath the hanging tiffany lamp. A waiter strode by, displacing enough air to wake the pages.

"You were the creative one," Bonniah said. "You wrote stories and had me read them out loud to you. You said that by hearing the words it helped you to better understand which ones belonged and which ones didn't."

Sarah held her sister's gaze, but her eyes had a flattened quality to them that suggested she was somewhere else. It seemed to Bonniah that Sarah had anticipated this very exchange and had already moved on, leaving her to scamper behind, as so often happened when they were children.

"You didn't ask me to come to Seattle just to go up the Space Needle with you, did you, Sarah?" Bonniah said, forcing a smile to camouflage her vexation.

You always smile to avoid getting to the point. You're a hopeless enabler when it comes to your sister.

"No, of course not, Bonnie," Sarah said, waking from a dream.

Bonniah stared across the table at her sister.

A year ago, Sarah had purportedly married a mystery man, a "giant," she had called him. No announcement, no wedding invitation, no pictures, no evidence of this Tanek Oleski anywhere, no sign of any man, in fact, much less a husband, anywhere on Sarah's person, handbag, car, apartment.

From the moment Bonniah had landed in Seattle something had seemed terribly out of kilter. At the airport she had failed to recognize her sister.

Sarah had aged markedly in the eighteen months since they had last seen each other. Her long chestnut hair had turned gray and wide and crinkly, as though suspended in electrified air. Something had tainted those once lively blue eyes, and the toxin had spread to the rest of her, leaving her skin thirsting and lined haphazardly about the eyes and mouth.

Perhaps what had most alarmed Bonniah was Sarah's utter disregard for her appearance. She wore no makeup. She looked like an aging hippie in her big formless gray dress, blue poncho and black sneakers, acquisitions from the local thrift shop, no doubt. Where was the vitality and purpose of movement, the Amazonian stride that had been emblematic of the Sarah Bonniah had so admired despite her sister's sporadic bouts with demons?

But what should she have expected? Something like this had happened before, after Sarah's last rehab, when her doctor had put her on Klonopin, the *Zombie Drug*, as Sarah had called it.

"I'm sorry, Bonnie."

"Sorry?"

Because you and Darren detest each other? Because I'm the one trapped in the middle? Because you dreamed up a little girl and a giant and tried to pass off your fantasy as reality? Are you sorry about that, Sarah? Is that what you are finally going to get around to telling me?

Maybe Sarah really was disordered the way Darren had meant it, intrinsically disordered, Darren the attorney who saw things others did not. Sarah could no longer hold her sister's gaze. She looked down at her hands instead, as if they were holding something she was incapable of releasing.

"I did want you to see Puget Sound and Mt. Rainier from the Space Needle," Sarah said, glancing up with a sad smile. "And the mountain ranges and the whole city. One huge breathing animal, Bonnie. I did want you to see it with me, yes."

Bonniah shook her head, resisting her sister's sentimentality.

"You once asked me what kind of woman I wanted to be," Bonniah said. "You asked me that because you never thought Darren was right for me. Maybe he's not the ideal husband, but you don't have such a great track record yourself. The question you should be asking is, what kind of woman do *you* want to be, Sarah?"

She waited for Sarah to respond, but Sarah bowed her head and resumed the study of her hands.

"My God, Sarah, if you're having trouble coming out and saying it, I'll do it for you. So things haven't quite worked out for you, have they? You're all alone again. I have an idea! Why don't I go ahead and be the good sister? I will divorce Darren, who doesn't know how to love a woman anyway, in your opinion, and I'll come live with you. I'll make sure you take all your meds and that you stay out of trouble. We'll go to the movies and museums together. We'll visit all the sights, volunteer at the soup kitchen. We'll grow old together, Sarah, two quaint little old ladies. Is that your ideal scenario, big sister? Is that what you want from me?"

Bonniah felt herself on the verge of trembling. She took a couple of deep breaths and looked away. She knew that if Sarah were to break then and there, she would rise from her seat and rush to embrace her.

But Sarah never broke. She had never seen her sister cry, she realized, even when they learned of the fatal accident that had stolen their parents from them. Whatever faint aura of nostalgia or sentimentality had hovered about Sarah evaporated as she listened to Bonniah's words.

"What is going on, Sarah?"

Bonniah held up the stapled pages and let them drop on the table in front of Sarah.

"My marriage is a bigger mess today because I'm here with you."

"Bonnie, I'm trying."

"What are you *trying*, Sarah? Some new hallucinogen?"

Sarah tried to smile.

Bonniah sighed as she felt that familiar thorny pain in her heart whenever the memory of loss overshadowed her. She wanted to leave. No, not just leave. She wanted to get up and run away. Run away and not look back.

Without thinking she gripped the table edge with both hands. An enormous unknown was descending upon her, like heavy black clouds. She didn't know how to be in that moment.

Just be, then, just be.

Something Sarah had once said.

Just be.

Bonniah took several slow deep breaths. She waved her hand at something or at nothing.

"That picture hanging over your bed?"

Sarah looked up. "The Sacred Heart," she said.

"Oh..."

Sarah gazed at Bonniah with unsettling intensity.

"I saw a tattoo like that, a heart encircled by thorns. It was on the limo driver's right hand."

Sarah smiled the way Bonniah loved.

"I was going to get off the plane and go back to Darren. I am so tired of battling with him, Sarah. I knew you would understand. I was ready to get up and leave, go back to him, when a woman appeared and sat down in the seat next to me. I could not make myself move. She turned and smiled at me, the way you just did. I felt as if you were there on the plane with me, and I knew I had to see you. I haven't handled this all that well, I know, and I'm sorry, but now you have to tell me why I'm here."

Sarah disappeared behind her closed eyes. Then came the tear that seemed almost unreal to Bonniah.

"Sarah, you're crying."

Sarah shook her head and took the stapled sheets and slowly scanned them, her frown deepening. She handed the sheets back to Bonniah. The sisters stared at each other, prisoners of all that had yet to be revealed.

"All this time I could not decide whether Tanek was real. Until now. When did he die, Sarah?"

THOUGH SHE DIDN'T EXPECT to ever see him again, she was disappointed when a different limo driver was waiting at Newark Airport to pick her up. She would have asked him about the tattoo, what the heart entangled in thorns had meant to him the day it became part of his skin, what it meant to him now.

The new driver looked to be in his mid-seventies, stiff, correct and courteous. His aloofness reminded her a little of Darren. He had the look of a man who once moved easily among prosperities and pleasures, a man of former means and influence, a man who had one day been visited by catastrophe.

Not once did he glance in the rearview mirror to assess her that she could tell. It was October, late in the afternoon and the sky was overcast. The darkness spilled with increasing ease into the days now, so why was she wearing sunglasses? Didn't he wonder? Had she become invisible finally, even to older men?

At the airport in Seattle, she had urged Sarah to go back to the apartment to get some rest. She would call her every day, she promised.

She had a clear purpose now. She knew the kind of woman she wanted and needed to be. She told Sarah she would return to Seattle next month, before Thanksgiving.

Remarkably, Sarah did as she was told. She went back to her apartment, and Bonniah had lots of time alone to think before departure. She spent a good portion of that time locked in a stall in the Ladies Room sobbing.

"Miss? Lady, are you alright?"

It was the voice of a young teenaged girl tapping on the stall door.

"Brittany, get over here!"

"But Mom..."

Bonniah wiped her face with toilet paper and put on her sunglasses. She listened to the teen and her mother walk out of the Ladies Room in a clash of loud whispers.

At dusk the large brightly lit house looked enchanted. Darren's car sat parked in the driveway. It surprised her that Darren would be home this early. Bonniah tread carefully between the glowing lanterns lining the brick walkway. The driver followed with her bag in hand and placed it on the front door landing.

"Goodnight," he said and turned to leave, his back stiffening visibly.

"Oh, but here, please," she said extending her hand.

"No need. It has already been taken care of."

He bowed slightly and turned once again to leave.

"Mr. Burns?"

He winced as he pivoted to face her, his hand reflexively rising to address the sudden stab of pain in his lower back. He regarded the woman with barely suppressed displeasure as she approached him.

Bonniah removed her sunglasses. Her eyes were pink and swollen. She stared at the man's saturnine face, illumined by the golden light of the walk lamps.

"Mrs. Ackerley, your husband appears to be home. You should let him know you have arrived."

She shook her head.

"Oh, but don't you see, Mr. Burns, my sister is dying."

She heard the words for the first time, and heard them again and again as if shouted from a great distance, from the Cascade Mountains, from Puget Sound, from the saturated city streets. The words in all their ghastly authority chasing her in circles, round and round the Space Needle observation deck, spinning her round and round.

For a moment, overcome with dizziness, she thought she was going to collapse. She looked at Mr. Burns and steadied herself. He was different now. A different man stood before her, his hard shell cracked and peeling away. He looked pensive, concerned. She imagined Sarah seeing that very look on Tanek's face and knew why she had fallen in love with him.

Mr. Burns smiled though his eyes were heavy with sadness. He hesitated a moment before taking Bonniah's hand. He held her hand between his own two hands and gave the impression he understood her predicament, the circumstances of her marriage, the kind of man she was married to.

"I am sorry, Mrs. Ackerley. I truly am, but this is all temporary, is it not? And we do the best we can in the meanwhile."

She wanted to run after Mr. Burns as he was driving away. She wanted to be sitting in the back seat of his limo, going wherever he went. But who would be there for Sarah?

When she entered the kitchen and smelled the lingering odor of Chinese food and saw the bowl he had used to eat his dinner in the sink filled with soapy water and an unfinished glass of red wine on the countertop, she wondered if Lena Sparks—at least the one she had conjured—could even exist in Darren's world.

Why that occurred to her then, she did not know, but she was now certain that her husband's eyes were incapable of seeing women like the one that had haunted her imagination.

In the attic she found Darren stooped over a corner of the diorama making final adjustments. He pretended not to notice her. He stood up straight and loomed over the battlefield like an indifferent titan.

Bonniah noted the fuller ranks of blue and gray. Darren had added thousands of miniscule warriors over the weekend. He must have stayed up very late each night arranging them. Their increased numbers lent to the battlefield a deeper broader dimension of tragedy.

"It's spectacular, Darren."

He did not feign surprise as he turned toward her. She felt him smile inwardly. He was happy, she realized. She was there to share with him the culmination of a four-year passion, and she wondered what would happen to their marriage.

"The demands of scale, of having to surrender to those demands. That was the most difficult thing. Do you remember the diorama we saw at Gettysburg several years ago, before I began this? A tourist attraction, beautifully inaccurate, certainly not without purpose and merit. I knew I wanted something closer to the truth. I added one hundred and twenty-eight square feet to their six-hundred and forty. I reduced the size of the combatants from their twenty-five-millimeter representations to six millimeters. And still it was not enough. To better understand the scale of this event—for example, to better grasp the physics of thousands of infantry moving across three quarters of a mile in the open field—I would have needed to increase the overall size of the theater between two to threefold."

He peered at her. "But I am not entirely disappointed."

His inner smile shone through to the surface ever so briefly, cutting Bonniah. Even when he is being good with her...

Oh, Darren.

"Look there," he said with sharp eyes, pointing to a sloping area just south of the town. "This is what I was referring to, the difficulty of getting to the truth. There is where it was all decided finally. On the third day of battle Lee ordered Longstreet to send 12,500 infantry nearly a mile over open fields against the heart of the Union line dug in along Cemetery Ridge, what we know as Pickett's Charge.

"There, you see that low stone wall? That is the place they call *The Angle*. Some of the Confederates managed to come all the way across and breach that wall, but they quickly became embroiled in bloody hand-to-hand combat and were repulsed. In the end it may have been Lee's arrogance, or mental fatigue, or misguided faith, or something altogether different that produced this epic disaster. How can we know? Can we ever know another's heart and mind? The Confederates suffered over fifty percent casualties. Their fate was sealed that day."

He stared at *The Angle*, observing the exhausting bloody horror as if through a time lens. He shook his head.

"Look at these hills and pastures, the roads, the buildings. The tiny military units that from our bird's eye view could almost be confused for flower beds. How peaceful it can all seem, if we choose not to look closely. From our perspective all appears still, nothing has yet happened. We can imagine this place having been for centuries free of the sound and fury of war and the stench of death.

"If Lee, a good man by all accounts, had stopped to think more deeply about life, about the fathers and sons and husbands and brothers under his command, about the call to something greater than mutual butchery and dismemberment—this man who is said to have prayed to God each and every day—he might have turned his army around. They might all have gone home to their families. But he did the opposite, Bonniah. He sent his men marching into hell... Perhaps he was tired of it all and wished to end it one way or another. Perhaps, in the end, he felt he had no choice."

She had never heard him speak like this. There was no response now she could give to this part of him. It grieved her to the core, this feeling of lost opportunity. She understood too well the cost of what she was about to say.

"Sarah's dying."

Darren took a deep breath and made a strange blowing motion with his mouth, as if he had just bit into a burning hot pepper. He scanned the battlefield with an anxious expression, as though he had just heard the first shot fired and could not locate its source, as though he, not Lee, had had the power all along but had missed the opportunity to prevent catastrophe.

He moved to the other side, to the west side, pointing again to Cemetery Ridge, but this time from Lee's vantage point.

"From here it should have become clear to him, the exhausting futility and horror that awaited his men. The merciless guns up on Cemetery Hill and along the ridge. But the inexorable might of destiny may have left him powerless to change the course of events."

He turned around. Something of the boy who once told her there was no one like her stared at her, suspended between then and now.

"Darren, Sarah's pregnant."

"What? You said she was dying!"

"I'm not lying to you. She has Stage 4 ovarian cancer."

She thought she detected *I'm not buying it* somewhere in the space that separated them, but it could be her, her inability to understand or to have herself understood.

"She was having abdominal pains. She thought she had IBS and went to see the doctor finally, but finally was too late."

Darren was staring at her as though she were pointing a musket at his face. She could not imagine what he was thinking. She did not want to know.

"The doctor said she has nine months to a year if they do nothing. With extensive surgery and chemotherapy two years, maybe, but they would have to remove her uterus. The baby is seventeen weeks old..."

"Where's the father?"

"He died not knowing she was pregnant."

Bonniah stared at Darren. What could he be thinking?

Finally, he turned back to his battlefield and began to thoughtfully trace the blue of Willoughby Run with his index finger, as if cooling himself in the tributary.

"Sarah asked if I would be the baby's legal guardian."

Darren lifted his hands in mild exasperation.

"Sarah sleeps around and—"

"Stop it! It wasn't like that. He was an older man, a good man, a survivor. They fell in love. He gave Sarah her one and only child. Imagine, after so many years, at her age. Some would say it's a miracle."

"A miracle? She's going to die, you just said so, and now this baby—"

"Darren, please. Please stop. Listen to me, please. I know you can't love me the way you've wanted to, or the way I've wanted you to. There are places in you I can't go because you won't let me. I'm not blaming you. We decided it would be better this way, the two of us. Maybe this was all a mistake, but for thirty years now—thirty years, my God—we've built a life together, raised a wonderful daughter and son. You once told me there was no one like me. We were so young. I thought that was your way of saying I love you...

"But what I've come to understand is that you *need* me. And maybe for you love and need are one and the same. But I haven't been that girl for a very long time now, and if you care for me, Darren, you have to accept that."

In a soft voice he said, "I didn't make a mistake. What I said all those years ago was true, is still true."

Bonniah hesitated, because of what he said, because of how hard this all was.

"She's going to name her Bonniah," she said, her voice breaking. "We're going to call her Bonnie."

She tried to find Darren's eyes but he hid them from her. Her legs felt tingly as she took several steps toward the stairs. She stopped at the southwest corner of the battlefield, turned around and went back to him.

He was trying to be the valiant soldier. It hurt her to see it. It made her tremble inside. For a moment she thought she was going to cry. Then his right hand, like a slow, weak pendulum, began to tap his leg.

Was he aware of what he was doing?

She followed the hand's hypnotic motion and imagined the thorn-ringed heart settling over its skin.

She took his hand in hers and kissed it where the heart had imprinted itself.

When she was gone Darren held his hand up, as though it had been shattered by a musket ball, and cast a troubled gaze over the battlefield.

Venere, Venere

OH, HE IS SOMETHING ELSE, let me tell you, sitting erect and supernaturally endowed with powers like some lesser god behind the wheel of his CL550 luxury coupe.

See the big tuna thighs cooling in the frosty effluvium issuing from the dashboard vents.

See the tightly wound woman to his right, legs crossed gazing out the passenger side window.

See how her defiant flank and slightly raised left shoulder exert a vexing pressure against his right eye.

He counts three parked cars where the woman is looking. One two three lumps beneath the ghostly nightlights. Go ahead, sneak-watch her squeezing herself against the shivers, she's so cold. Take in the familiar slender fingers pressing the soft pale flesh of her bare arm, the long crimson fingernails.

Shivering for love is what she's doing, let's not kid ourselves. That pale shivering form hungry for love, that's right, the kind he knows how to package and deliver.

Deluded fellow, wouldn't you say, this attributing to women his erratic lusts? These notions of mutual desire dangling before him like sugarplums?

A part of him knows it, so he ramps up the AC, and not surprisingly, the woman flinches. He enjoys her discomfort, finds the virile roar of the cold blast that is washing over her delightful—yes, sometimes he likes using the word *delightful*, but only in his head if someone else is present, or out loud when he's alone talking to himself.

But why such modesty?

He smiles a little uncomfortably remembering the once chubby Kenny Mars of long ago and how that little fella worked his way out of hellish childhood to become the man he now is.

The MAN he is now.

Mars, The MAN, shakes (not stirs) imaginary water from his head like a frat boy after May finals being hose-sprayed in the frat house driveway by a buzzed coed he's about to... hose?

Good times, good times.

The woman further constricts. He pays closer attention and finds himself constricting too. Wishes so hard he could just laugh like a barroom lumberjack and just be done with all the stress bunching up in the shrinking space they share, but he can't. What happens when you start thinking too much is this, precisely this, gosh darn it.

He drums his thighs lightly, makes himself think the whole thing kind of funny, actually, and wants to laugh real bad, but it gets all clogged up in his throat like stubborn phlegm, so he undoes one more shirt button.

Her silent hand moves over the air and disappears for a moment and the passenger side window descends, inviting in the simmering vegetable night. Almost immediately Mars feels an oily prickle on his neck. Not anger that stirs him suddenly, not really, but an agitation of the blood, a primal urge to carry her off to a field, a wanting—an *intense* wanting, make no mistake—to spread her out on the grass and make her cry out his name in equal measures of pain and pleasure.

Ken! Ken! Oh, Kenny!

Yes, that's right, in equal measures.

He studies her uncooperative form, the expensively done hair come partly undone. His hand rises uncertainly, maybe to touch her flesh, but he cannot do it. He palms his knees and squeezes them until his hands ache. He grips the steering wheel as if it were on the verge of spinning away into the stratosphere, leaving him behind without direction. He leans forward, his back straight as a block toy, and glares at the dreary parking lot.

And because this horseshit must not stand, he flops back against the seat and exhales an archetypal Mars admonition.

"Norma, Norma. For the love of God, our baby just got married."

The woman presses her lips together and shoulders the latest indignity. The little blue hatchback she's looking at sprouts metal wings and flies away.

ODDLY ENOUGH, the golden girl sat all alone on the groom's side of the church. No one spoke a word to her.

In the reception hall she looks like royalty, but the trouble-making kind. She's wearing sparkly gold stilettos and a short silky dress that slides like sun-kissed water over her thighs and salient bottom. Her hair is dark gold—as though rinsed with an added drop of blood—and drawn tight against her perfectly shaped head. I, for one, wonder who put her in our midst.

She glitters with severity and strangeness from head to toe, and Mars has been aiming to make her acquaintance from the moment he first saw her in church.

With martini in hand, he moves from table to table slapping backs, laughing, and making small talk, all the while eyeing and evaluating the golden girl as if he were an impromptu judge of the female form.

As father of the bride, he claims first rights of impertinence and is not one to squander such rare opportunities. The most naïve among the guests interpret the pair's engagements on the dance floor as sanitary exhibitions of roguish fun, atmosphere enhancers. She must be a niece, or a friend of the daughter, they suggest to one another. But those remain in the minority. It doesn't take a cynic to embrace a darker interpretation.

While slow-dancing to *You Are the Sunshine of My Life* she looks deep into his eyes and matter-of-factly confesses to preferring mature married men to young untested males.

He replies, "Well now, pardon my French, but that's just the biggest pile of horseshit I've ever heard," prompting her to throw back her head and produce a stunning guttural laugh that causes his mouth to open and his attention to be fully trained on her smooth-muscled throat. The smell of gin on her breath makes him inch closer.

In mock seriousness he accuses her of duplicity and of abiding by some treacherous feminist agenda designed to tear down men of consequence and stature such as himself.

She appears oddly unaffected by what he says, as if he has spoken to her in a dead language.

At dusk, in a grove of sugar maples just beyond sight of the country club, and barely above the shrill chorus of vibrating male cicada membranes, he says. "What's your name, sweetheart?"

"Zin," she says in a detached way.

"You mean like the flower, Zinnia?" he says with a dreamy grin as she unbuttons his shirt. She's counting *Zin* for each button, *Zin, Zin, Zin*, down to the last one.

Nice touch, enthralling in a creepy way, and a properly unique thank you for delivering the goods, as per feeding of the four-hundred, limitless bar, grossly overpriced help (i.e., planner, florist, photographer, band, limo), happy bride snuggly fitted into $12,000 gown smiling-dancing with her scrotum-aching grinning groom.

Was it too much? Why dwell on such things? Given the current progression? Would have to say money well spent, well spent.

So, whose idea? Who thinks along such lines? His evil twin? Ha-ha. Brilliant minds do think alike.

Quick-check most probable genius list: Jack Huff, Len Gilliam, Blake Manfred, etcetera? Team effort, etcetera? Hmm, whoever. Or is it whomever? Whatever whoever whomever. I dub thee *Sir Genius of Desire*, for thou hath procured thy liege the most perfect blend of flower, fruitcake, and whore.

And rightly so, my liege, and rightly so.

Mars performs small unsuccessful maneuvers to kiss the lithe creature's mouth.

"Who are you?" he mutters smiling in frustration. "Who sent you, Golden Sunshine?"

She's humming along until the trousers' zipper gets snagged on his boxers' fly. Mars wonders why she doesn't just yank everything down in one fell swoop but is too absorbed to say anything. Her focus, her attention to detail. Remarkable, remarkable.

However...

A pounding noise gives him pause as his trousers fall to his ankles and Golden Sunshine takes a step back. Before he can turn his head, he is tackled to the ground.

"What the fug!" he cries after going down on his chest with a *hooumph!*

I've got him in a full nelson. He's thrashing and flopping like a toppled wildebeest, his snout dragging across the sod rooting for oxygen. I'm pressing down hard, pulling on his arms, stressing his rotator cuffs.

And ah, whew, how the stink of his hair gel makes me want to puke, makes vodka-flavored spit spray from my mouth onto his head as I'm shouting, "You foul bitch! You foul stinking bitch!" (Rebukes that trigger in Mars shocks of déjà vu.)

The world is in full tilt as he realizes it's me. His body goes limp. Without releasing my hold, I pause, gasping for air. *Oh geez, come on, Lesser, you've been through worse than this.*

We're both catching our breath, two overweight middle-aged men. Am I really doing this? If so, why? My hold relaxes just a tad as I take stock of the moment.

Mars realizes it's no dream—no variation of a recurring nightmare—and begins counting to ten in his head but then waits to twelve before he starts to buck.

I'm no fool, and having anticipated his move, having a shared history to call upon, I reinforce my hold, jerk our bound torsos up off the ground in brief suspension, and slam us back onto the ground with a ribcage-shattering double *oomph!*

Now I'm working his rotators in earnest and pushing the side of his face deeper into the dewy ground. He starts crying out, "Ow, ow, ow!"

Am I surprised? No! Because when the going gets tough and so on, well, this is what he does. When it really comes down to it, Ken Mars has always been a pansy.

By all rights I should be the one yelling *Ow, ow, ow!* given the left lower back strain and shooting pains down my ass and hamstring, up my neck and shoulder, the damn migraines, waves of nausea, overall daily malaise and general discontent... But you won't hear me crying out *Ow, ow, ow!* Real men don't do that.

My body desperately wants relief and a return to more rational pursuits (e.g., issue a stern warning, relax the murderous hold, exchange a mature word or two), but my half-spun head is yelling, *To hell with that shit!*

Marshalling iron strength of mind, body and purpose, I release him. He flops over. Our eyes lock for a moment. I smash his red face with my forearm and collapse over him like a blanket of ham.

Dazed as much by the blow as by the incongruity of his predicament, Mars spends a few moments tasting blood and arranging fragments of understanding before slurring in my ear, "God almighty, Ned, what the hell happened to finding Jesus?"

Did I just stop breathing? No, not this time. Breathe, Lesser, that's it, breathe.

My limp wet mass begins to shift. Gasping and lightheaded, I peel myself off Mars. I'm kneeling by his side like a dazed soldier, one hand over my heart that's going *thump, thump, thump,* one hand pressed against my lower back, my ass heavy on my heels. Mars is staring at me, marveling, breathing almost as hard as I am.

I'm sucking air like someone dragged from the sea in the nick of time. I feel soft, gray and swollen. My eyes are stinging and I'm seeing double. My body bobs faintly as I gaze half blind and without hope at the trees and the darkening sky. The cicadas are either loving or hating us and their membranes are vibrating louder than ever. My arms drop and hang dead at my sides like hooked butcher meat.

Finally, in a delicate voice that surprises me I say, "You never did deserve her."

I can't bear to look at his face when I say it. I lift myself into a crouch and tap my chest three times. Mars is thinking something constructive ought to be said as he watches me totter in the direction of the reception hall, but the words elude him.

LYING ON HIS BACK, Mars recalls how he used to pin me to the filthy industrial carpet in our dorm lounge and how he used to whisper in my ear, "The Lesser man always loses, Lesser," as a kind of signature before releasing me. And how I, incredibly, always came back for more, cocksure and borderline deranged, laughing at him like some bloodied but unbowed Hollywood swashbuckler, like *I* had just kicked *his* ass.

As exhausting as that aspect of me was for him to deal with, it was the main reason he asked me to be the best man at his wedding all those years ago, that Lesser *Never Say Die* credo leaving quite the impression on him. And also, that I was the little brother he kept in a headlock, which made me handy to have around.

But then came *The Real World*, and in Mars's view, it wasn't long before I, being the Lesser, would take a cold, hard look at my life and find it wanting. *Wanting* being the key word here or *want* in all its derivations and interpretations and in its most visceral form becoming the guiding force in his, and therefore, everybody else's daily life.

In his mind what I wanted was what he had—his job, his house, his car, and most amusingly to him, his wife. That's what he had probably thought for a long time, since the day I set eyes on Norma senior year, and it ate me up to think he was right about that last part.

Pursuing his train of thought, I understood that because I couldn't have what I wanted that was his, I sought out and secured the next best thing, his sister.

We never addressed this other than through innuendo, nor did he ever try to talk Kitty out of loving me because, well, that's just not the way love works, is it? Nobody could talk Kitty out of loving me, my poor dear Kitty. Even Mars knew that.

He also knew I would treat his sister right, be to her the faithful husband he chose not to be to his wife, and if marrying Kitty made me feel like I had tipped the scales a little bit back in my favor, so long as Kitty was relatively happy, or at least not overtly miserable, then so be it. That was an acceptable scenario for Mars, who has always fancied himself a strong proponent of family harmony.

For a while, things were good but went to less, our marriage having peaked in the Maldives during our honeymoon. When our kids went off to college I started drinking and then I stopped being a husband in the complete sense of the word. Not an unfaithful husband, mind you, but a rigorously celibate one.

Kitty tried to be understanding but grew increasingly dejected and Mars felt compelled to intervene. I tried to imagine what the meeting Mars had proposed would be like while on my way home from work stuck in bumper-to-bumper traffic on the Parkway.

I pictured Mars standing before a bathroom mirror rehearsing the man-to-man talk he was going to have with me and envisioned Kitty sitting anxiously by my side on the sofa couch in our living room, Mars breaking the ice with some marriage-themed joke before getting down to business, me at a total loss for words the entire time, as though I'd forgotten I had a tongue in my mouth, and my gaze drifting away from them both toward the door, the exit, the way out, and meanwhile Mars's words fading, fading until a white dove settled on the hood of my stalled-in-traffic car and spoke to me. It looked at me through the windshield with big kaleidoscopic eyes, its wings spread wide like flames of white fire, and spoke to me in the voice of an angel, "God is good. Good is God."

Later, after Mars told his little icebreaker joke, and before he could get on a roll, that is what I said to him, "God is good. Good is God."

He laughed uncertainly suspecting I had somehow parlayed his little icebreaker joke into one of my own. Then I told him and Kitty all about the white dove with the big kaleidoscopic eyes and fiery wings and what the dove had said to me in the voice of an angel.

When Kitty, moved to tears by my words, revealed that she had been praying for this very miracle for months and that today God had answered her prayer, Mars was forced to swallow all the meticulously crafted pointers and recommendations he had rehearsed in front of his bathroom mirror.

"This is nice," he kept saying and nodding. "This is nice."

Yes, and now *this*, he's thinking. Of all the three-hundred and sixty-five days of the year for the brother-in-law to pull a Jekyll and Hyde act, did he have to choose Kaitlyn's wedding day to ruin his three-thousand-dollar Armani suit?

That is what Mars is thinking. Believe me when I say that is exactly what he's thinking.

He sits up and licks the blood from his lower lip, which tastes like a salted penny. In spite of everything, he can't help but smile as he thinks of me.

That son of a bitch always did sport a pair of hefties.

He frowns as he remembers Golden Sunshine. How much of this unflattering spectacle had she observed?

His stomach begins to growl. He lowers his head and listens attentively. Somewhere in there, there's a message. He squats into a three-point stance, knees bent, rear end parallel to the ground, right hand fingertips kissing the ground, thighs and buttocks coiled tight and ready to spring in a burst of awesome power. He glances to his left at twenty-year old me holding down left guard, three-point stance, mirror image, the two of us primed to explode and plow up that defensive front.

Mars feels a rush of nostalgia as he blasts a single imperious fart for old times' sake.

He stands up, feeling some relief but quickly becomes restless and vaguely disappointed. He rubs his forehead, coaxes his brain. He feels for the card in his shirt pocket and carries it like a slice of warm cheese to the nearest lantern where he reads, *Zinnia Peck, MD, Psychiatrist, Author.*

He turns the card over: *Call me Zin.*

Or did she mean, *Call me, Zin?*

Or was she playing with his head, mining him for raw material?

Mars slips the card in his wallet, right behind the family photos, and opts for a trip to the Men's Room before heading back to the *Parents of the Bride* table.

SHE DOESN'T ASK about the busted lip or the green smears on his jacket and pants. She squeezes herself and looks out at the parking lot.

Gee, Ned, thanks for everything, my busted lip, throbbing head, ruined Armani, and oh, yeah, my dislodged aching jaw. Damn, Ned. Can you lighten up for once? Jeremy Christmas!

Mars works hard at being optimistic. Day after day he works at seeing the glass half full. It's something any half-brained person would tell you, you ought to do. You have to work at it, but people can be such a royal pain in his ass that half the time they get him off kilter and sometimes he's expending way too much energy because of these stupid fugs—

Whoa! Whoa there! See that? So the trick is to get back on kilter without expending too much precious energy.

On the wall behind his desk at work, next to the family portrait and *Executive of the Year* plaque, hangs an elaborately wood-framed poster depicting King Arthur laughing his ass off surrounded at round table by laughing knights and the words *Laughter Is the Best Medicine* appearing below the image in *Olde English* font.

His son Danny took the liberty to put it up while Mars was out to lunch. Mars came back, saw it, cursed, was ready to tear it down and fire somebody thinking one of the assholes in his department (Ray-Ray the Zealot?) was sending some kind of message when Danny walks in from taking a leak. "Like it, Dad?"

It grew on him and is now indispensable.

After a rough day Mars likes to swivel around and stare at King Arthur until the smile, he's forcing breaks into laughter. He sits wondering why it's so hard for people to embrace such a simple principle.

If he's learned one thing in life, it's that people enjoy shoving their self-indulgent horseshit craziness in your face, and only intestinal fortitude and maintaining a healthy perspective can keep a man properly centered and productive.

It may not be obvious to some (me, for instance), but Mars fancies himself contemplative and analytical by nature. These attributes form the foundation from which to manage his workers, disseminate his expertise, provide guidance, delegate effectively, ensure the success of that all-important max return on investment, and do it all with a smile, always a smile.

Why is smiling so hard for some people?

At the same time, too much thinking can be counter-productive and irksome. When Mars falls into that trap, unwittingly—always unwittingly—it is because he has crossed a certain threshold. That's when the dry rot begins, that awful taste in his mouth. At that point his perspective dims and the spear tip of fear begins to poke him.

He doesn't talk about it, never has, doesn't even like writing about it, though he now and then feels compelled to jot down words as a form of relief. He jots down, *Get poster like the one Danny got me. Hang on wall behind desk in study.*

That way, anytime he wants, he can swivel around at home too and behold King Arthur's laughing-his-ass-off face and say it out loud, *Laughter Is the Best Medicine,* then force himself to laugh. Yes, force, if need be. Smile first, then laugh, because doesn't every laugh have to begin with a smile?

One evening he was in the kitchen making himself a fat Ham and Swiss heavy on the tomatoes, onions, tabasco and mayo. He heard a noise and saw a man walking up the stairs to his bedroom. His stomach lurched at the sight and at what such a development might portend.

His mouth filled with dry rot so fast that he had to wash it out with whiskey. He gargled, whipped the whiskey around in his mouth with his tongue, and swallowed every drop before he could work up the courage to go upstairs.

Of course, there was no one there, no intruder in the sheets, no rapist, no killer, no nothing. Norma was herself all alone with all the lights on, propped on two pillows, reading one of her damn books.

What are you reading? he said with a look of suspicion. She gazed at him as if at a delinquent child. *Beloved,* she said. Geez, you and your romance novels, he said. No, not *that* Beloved, she said, but he had no idea what she was talking about or any interest in asking her to elaborate. He was just relieved the stranger wasn't in *his* bed pleasuring *his* wife.

It began to happen twice a week on alternate days, mostly Tuesdays and Thursdays, but also Mondays and Wednesdays. Each time he took a big swig of whiskey and walked up the stairs just to make sure. Norma was always reading a damn book or grading papers or on her side sleeping.

He didn't want it to become part of his routine, one of those obsessive-compulsive things, and he knew it was all in his head, but he just had to make sure every single time. It was starting to get on his nerves.

So he came up with a solution. Whenever he senses the stranger's presence, he imagines him standing at the foot of the bed, and Norma watching the stranger with mild interest. Once that part is set, he imagines Norma covering her mouth to suppress a guffaw immediately before the stranger looks down to discover his manhood has been swapped out for a lima bean.

THE SCENE IS ARGUABLY *untoward* (yes, *untoward* being another of Mars's secret words), but personally *delightful* as all heck, and just so encouraging and consoling that he finally is able to let out a laugh. Feeling better now, he licks the bad taste from his teeth and lists his head toward Norma as if to release water from his ear (those wild coeds with their hoses!).

His mouth flexes into an arduous smile as he sets the AC to low and raises the passenger side window. All things considered, he is a reasonable man. The hum of the dual turbo engine makes his body tingle as his beloved Mercedes CL550 leaps out of the parking lot.

The jolt makes Norma grind her teeth. She crosses her legs the opposite way and folds her hands on her lap. Her lovely knees glow intermittently in the shifting night shadows as they ride the dark, featureless road. Mars, still stinging more from his earlier aborted pleasure escapade than from my thrashing, finds himself suddenly aching to correct that vengeful disinterested way Norma has been receiving his love thing the last couple of years.

Maybe the night can still be salvaged, he thinks, but also wonders, did Golden Sunshine see Ned pancake his face?

Meanwhile, in the periphery of Norma's left eye Mars looms like a rumpled bulk one might find piled in the corner of an alley or against a damp-stained wall in an old warehouse. How is it possible? One day Ken Mars appeared in her life and swept her off her feet. Now he revolts her to the core.

I tell you it's true, though she's never confessed such a thing to me or anyone. But I know it to be true, trust me.

RECENTLY— or has it been at least a year? —she has begun to think about other men. Men in the neighborhood, in her social circle. Typically, they are safe, unattainable men. Dignified men. A retired newsman, for instance. A concert pianist. A widowed deacon from her church. They take turns conversing with her in the privacy of her head. Man to woman, woman to man. Sometimes the men stop talking to gaze fondly at her, or perhaps covetously.

She avoids talking about men to other women for fear she will be exposed. Kitty tells her all about my medical conditions, sexual quirks and mysterious journey into celibacy. But Norma has been of no help, responding with little more than platitudes and clumsy segues to other topics—Anne Tyler's latest novel, the grand opening of a new *Pottery Shack,* the heat wave, and so on.

That Kitty is unwilling to look at the world's filthy undergarments makes life just that much more problematic for Norma. Admittedly, there are times she envies Kitty's naiveté, that safe place she appears to inhabit in perpetuity, but it can make her, Norma, crazy.

Sometimes when Kitty is twittering away, she wants to press her hand over her sister-in-law's mouth and whisper, *Shush, Kitty! Just shush already!* and pour a long stream of truth in that porcelain white ear. She wants especially to tell her how miserable she is being married to her disgraceful brother.

Kitty's brother blights the car like an obscenity. His presence is like the stench of slow dying, and where the headlights peer far into the night, Norma sees him pinned beneath a younger woman, whimpering like an ape at the apex of pleasure.

"I'd like a drink," she says.

"A drink? Great idea!"

Mars begins to turn the car around.

"What are you doing?"

"Going to Danny's."

"I already told you I didn't want to go to Danny's."

"Of course, of course. Fine, I understand. Enough of the family for one day. I get it."

They drive in silence a few miles, Mars cogitating, turning at a traffic light, and heading north. In minutes they are pulling into another parking lot, the gravel crackling beneath the big tires like a hailstorm. Mars checks his watch.

"You know, we might run into one or two of the guests here," he says. He glances casually about the crowded lot, yawns, rolls his shoulders. "I mean, is that a problem?"

She stares at the bull profile, the familiar imperfections, the impending sag line of jowl and chin.

He pretends not to notice as he runs his index finger halfway around the steering wheel, spends a moment or two regarding his crotch, fingertip-taps his lips for a while, then turns his face and says, "We'll go in if you like. It's what you want, isn't it?"

The night stretches before her like a torture rack. She thinks of women with exotic names who castrate lovers and judges herself a coward by contrast. Tomorrow he will be on the golf course all day, and she will pull at her finger joints and neck hair and scratch the right side of her chin with the newly manicured fingernails of her left hand until her skin ignites, and as she walks to the bathroom for the ointment, she will imagine a knife and a perfect circle of blood on the kitchen floor surrounding her broken body like a gruesome corona.

But it doesn't have to be this way. Not anymore.

She enters the place with a casual sweeping glance, already having imagined the golden girl seated prominently on a stool sipping beer like a barroom baroness, her long legs on display for the viewing pleasure-torture of flesh-hungry men. But the girl is nowhere to be seen, not yet at least. Norma feels relief, but also a sense of having been cheated.

A martini, please. Mars orders a mug of stout to cut into that raving thirst and studies the various crude implements displayed on the planked wall behind Norma. He is succinct in his appraisal of the ambiance, and incidentally submits Kitty's name and mine hoping to gather information, but Norma doesn't bite.

Past Mars's right shoulder high on a wall is a television flashing that all too familiar shot of President Clinton and the darkhaired intern hugging in front of a bemused crowd. That's followed by a shot of a blue dress and commentary by Senator Orrin Hatch that no one can hear.

Mars downs the rest of his drink with a flourish of impatience, smiles, and excuses himself. She watches him negotiate a corner, playfully eluding a pigtailed waitress who is balancing a tray of drinks and flashing Mars a distressed smile.

Norma polishes off her martini like it's a glass of lemonade and studies the people clustered about the bar. A freckly, orange-haired waiter places a tall tapering glass of ale before her. She smiles broadly at the waiter with that engaging, but rarely seen now smile of hers, and when he turns and leaves all her attention is on the tall narrow glass and coping with the melancholy it is coaxing forth. She takes a deep breath and plunges into the tongue-teasing beverage and is almost immediately rewarded with a feeling close to but not quite abandon. She tilts forward, stretching her haunches, enjoying the pleasure the stretch gives her.

She gazes at the crowd, young, mostly, largely uninteresting, a typical Saturday night crew, she suspects. But a pale, shorthaired brunette at the bar catches her eye, not overly pretty, but lovely, a soft-featured translucent creature that flees the sun for climate-controlled spaces. She is speaking animatedly to an ordinary man, elevating him to a higher degree of relevance by virtue of her intense interest in him.

Intrigued, Norma studies the man, finds him composed in a spare, mysterious way.

She measures him top to bottom. He is slight, of mannequin proportions, with a clean angular face and a high forehead. His hair is pale yellow and cropped short to the sides of his head, rising up at a backward tilt on top, like a field of wheat against the wind. He is wearing khaki pants, a navy-blue polo shirt, and what appears to be an earring in his left earlobe. Yes, an earring with a pronounced glimmer. The observation triggers a scary-good sensation inside her, and she wonders, is he a musician, artist, a poet?

She intuits a special sensitivity, so when he turns his head, she is fully prepared to adopt the concentrated, mildly perturbed expression of a patron waiting for a companion who is taking way too long to appear.

The immediate thrill she experiences vanishes in an instant, though. She has, apparently, interrupted something dear to him, distracted him from precious moments of intimacy. Unsmiling, he turns back to the brunette. Norma surmises he is in love with her.

Norma-Norma raises the glass to her lips, peeking up from her drink like a schoolgirl and grateful no one else has taken notice of her silly game.

The man draws his wallet from his back pocket. Another man (the girl's boyfriend?) counters by reaching back to retrieve his own wallet, but it is an empty gesture that goes largely unacknowledged. The lovely pale brunette takes the unsmiling man's right arm in her hands and shakes it wistfully.

Is she pleading with him? No, she is gently chastising him. But why? What is it that she wants of him?

The man shakes his head, forces a smile, places bills on the bar counter as the bartender places another beer before him. The girl kisses the man on the cheek. The other man shakes his hand and embraces him awkwardly. The couple begin walking away, and the man is left alone sitting on a barstool.

The couple walk past Norma on their way to another place. The other man (the boyfriend?) inclines his head toward the lovely girl and asks her a question, but she is utterly removed, lost amid troubled thoughts, it seems, and Norma experiences a premonition of sadness. No, of sorrow.

She studies Mr. Lonesome at an angle. He is staring at a row of bottles shelved against the bar wall mirror—no, actually, he is staring at himself. She no longer sees the crowd but him alone and is puzzled as to why she should feel herself on the brink of tears.

He sips from his mug and licks foam from his lips, and Norma imitates him, sipping and licking. When he turns his head toward her, her hand flinches like a spastic wing, sending a splash of ale into the air. She dabs her mouth with a napkin and wipes the table. What a clown she is, how like a clown without her makeup.

She eyes the agitated liquid as she swallows, mindful that it go down without further incident. Then she sets the glass down and smiles faintly, finding steadiness in the examination of her long crimson fingernails. She flattens her left hand on the table and applies her right to it to keep it from rising to her capricious chin that is demanding to be scratched.

All the while, she is enduring Mr. Lonesome's steadfast gaze that is penetrating to her maddened heart. She is desperate for a diversion, a cigarette to hold in her hand, smoke to blow out her mouth... If only she smoked.

Norma coughs into her hand, and the hand forms a flimsy shield that dissolves like a vague notion, and she can't keep the stranger from peering into the mess she is, so inelegantly transparent, so much the see-through older woman.

She attempts to aggregate herself to the others, the people being watched by other people, the ones chatting away, the distracted waiters and waitresses plucking dollar bills and credit card trays and sweating glasses from table after table.

She fails. Mr. Lonesome has demolished the anonymity she has tried to construct for herself, and she doesn't know what to make of such power.

She is a mature woman, she tells herself, an educated woman, a teacher. The mother of four adults, six grandchildren.

And yet, that he is young enough to be her daughter's groom, or her own son, is irrelevant to her. What surprises her most is that she, Norma Mars, wants so desperately to be someone else entirely at this stage of her life.

But what is she thinking? How idiotic it all is! Very well then, have at it, take a long hard look at this unhappy and lonely aging woman. She lifts her head and finds herself gazing helplessly at the stranger in a tautness of mutual beholding. The loss of interest she was anticipating on his part never happens. There is no escape, she discovers. It is as if she is bound by a great volume of rising water awaiting the pronouncement of her fate while drowning in increments. Can he possibly know her limit? Can he determine the moment of her annihilation?

From out of the final breathless blur, he smiles in a kindly manner, and all the world seems to have changed. His mercy overwhelms her like a rush of oxygen, and she smiles as she turns away, her head afloat, her heart aflutter. She considers thanking him, but no, she must go now. She and Ken need to leave before the sea she is swimming in becomes too deep for light.

But there remains the matter of the phone call.

The thought has hovered in her mind like a trapped vapor. She stands up and walks with strained precision past the stranger, glancing back once to see if he is watching her. Already he has forgotten her. It is just as well.

She turns the corner where her husband nearly collided with the pigtailed waitress and enters a corridor that presents four doors and a narrow, recessed cubbyhole. She imagines Ken sitting on a toilet in the Men's Room feeling shortchanged, or honing his flirtation skills in the *Special Occasions* room, or asking some calculated question in the *Employees Only* room. Or maybe he just got as tired as she is of everything and decided to walk out the Emergency Exit.

She sits down on a horseshoe-shaped padded bench in the cubbyhole but cannot bring herself to call Kitty. Instead, she calls the club but quickly aborts the call when the *Special Occasions* door swings open and spits out a chunk of loud laughter along with an unusually dramatic young couple (he with the waist-length ponytail, she with the meaty tanned thighs) that stride past her as if she were invisible. Norma's left hand, which has developed a mind of its own in recent years, begins twisting a lock of neck hair as she listens to the fading chortles of men and a woman's rich lingering giggle.

She presses the phone against her forehead to dispel the worst thoughts. It's important she make the call, though she is presently not fully convinced she should be the one. It's not her sister, after all. It's his. But you marry a family, not an individual, Janice had reminded her on their way to the faculty lounge, the same day her colleague had given her the name of her divorce lawyer.

So, to be consistent, when I divorced Chuck, I divorced his entire family, Janice had explained with not a trace of remorse.

Those words were both alluring and troubling. Who wouldn't want a clean break, a new beginning? Why be constantly reminded of the unhappiest days of your life by all the familiar faces that populated that long period of misery?

That night she had tossed and turned for hours. At four in the morning, she got up, turned on the bathroom light, stood before the mirror and confirmed that she was, in fact, Norma, not Janice.

She was Norma and so had no choice, really. You don't cut ties with people you care about, divorce or not. She had to make the call because Kitty told her I had gone for a walk to clear my head but had not returned.

Norma had to make the call because her response to Kitty's veiled appeal for company and assurances was to kiss her sister-in-law on the cheek and walk out to the parking lot waving goodbye with self-absorbed Mars trailing behind like a heavy-footed stalker.

What had she been thinking? It was wrong not to have stayed with Kitty until I reappeared or somebody delivered me to my wife in whatever shape or form.

Maybe she is blowing things out of proportion. Maybe she has had one drink too many. In all likelihood, the man at the club will tell her everyone left the establishment with no issue and will seek assurances that she and her family and guests spent a most pleasant and memorable day at Maple Grove Country Club and that all her expectations had been exceeded, and please, if there's anything else we can do.

But what could have happened to Ned? Nothing, surely, she tells herself. Nothing, but that other thing... Oh, yes, that. That silly thing I said to her on the veranda at the reception. Our little secret, mine and Norma's. No one else need ever know. She will tease me about it, offer us a way out. We'll share a laugh at some point and then move on with our lives.

But Kitty... Wow, she had kissed her on the cheek and waved ta-ta and left her standing there like a waif while the workers were clearing tables and sweeping floors and thinking about getting home, and everybody else was saying, *Good night, what a grand wedding, that singer reminded me of, of, ah hell, can't remember, and oh, by the way, who was the blonde with the legs that just would not quit?*

She can call Kitty right now, but the act will just serve to highlight her moral failure, and certainly it will not matter anyway because Kitty this very moment is driving home with me sleeping it off in the passenger seat.

Right? Well...

She calls the club instead and grills the man on the phone. "What do you mean an ambulance arrived but you cannot tell me more?"

"I'm sorry, madam. I was given no details." Did he just stifle a yawn? "If you'd like directions to the hospital," he begins to say, but she cuts him off.

Now the stranger and his earring are blocking her way. Why is he looking at her like that? What does he want? She steps sideways. He mirrors her, softly, stepping in front of her again, like a dancer in a silent film.

On an impulse she glances down as if to sidestep a hidden trap, her eyes sweeping past his fly and down to the clean brown shoes and then back up brushing his pale gray eyes and then veering toward that remarkable earring and lingering there a moment or two.

She is about to ask him if he has lost the other one when a loud burst of laughter in *Special Occasions* reconnects her to the world of Mars.

Two joking women walk out and cross directly into the Ladies Room, but what she needs is someone rational to emerge from one of those four doors and get between her and the stranger or do something to make her forget the horrid, insouciant voice of that man on the phone and to silence the ambulance siren in her head and delete the whirling lights and maybe tell this oddball to get out of her damn way.

His eyes have become a predatory gray and it makes her wonder as she glances at the Emergency Exit door, is this what it has come to? Her life's sum total of disappointments and futilities ending with the abduction, rape and murder of a middle-aged woman, mother of four, grandmother of six?

The alien timbre of his voice takes her by surprise. "Please, please," he says, taking her forearm in his hands with exaggerated tenderness.

She looks at him, strangeness heaped upon strangeness, things tilting, ready to crash. She teeters on the verge of laughter, which she promptly rejects as though somehow Ken were behind this, directing the carnival. "I must go," she says but makes no effort to move.

He takes and lifts her hand, palm up, to his mouth. His lips are soft on her damp fingertips, his warm beer breath rolls into her palm. He closes his eyes and presses his afflicted mouth against the very center of her hand. The sweet tingling absurdity of the gesture momentarily wins her, but she snatches her hand away as she imagines herself tied to a chair in a damp, poorly lit basement.

She tenses when the stranger slips his hand into his pants pocket. A glossy silver business card appears inches from her face. She reads the name *Werther Maria Heilbronn, Company President* embossed in blue calligraphy. Along with the unlikely name and title, the suggestive but indeterminate words, *UrDream Novelty Imports*, and basic contact information.

She almost laughs as she imagines the fawning brunette and her ineffectual male companion along with Werther Maria Heilbronn, Company President, haggling over expenses in a small cramped room containing a water cooler, sixth grade iron-framed wood desks, and an outdated *National Geographic* map of the world tacked to the wall.

"You wish to say something to me?" he intones in a Germanic accent.

She ignores him but slips his card in her purse as she turns away. She hears him utter cryptically, "But why? I do not understand."

Norma marches past Mars on her way out of the pub, not sure where she is going or what she is doing.

"Hey!"

Mars fishes out his wallet and slams two twenties on the table and follows Norma out to the parking lot. He lunges off balance and grabs her by the arm and spins her around, hurting her shoulder.

"What the hell?" he shouts. The abrupt silence of the cicadas makes him feel targeted. Someone is watching him, the young couple that came out of the *Special Occasions* room.

Mars's irritation is smoothed away upon beholding a pair of juicy thighs crowned by a dazzling white miniskirt. He releases Norma's arm, smiles, and makes a dismissive, albeit reassuring, motion with his hand in the direction of the couple, as if divesting them of civic responsibility.

The couple climb into a black Ford Explorer and gaze intently at Mars as they drive by. The interrupted cicada chorus reasserts itself in the form of thousands of recriminations.

Norma walks back to the Mercedes holding her shoulder, but stops abruptly, her body tensing. Mars comes around to face her, careful not to touch any part of her. His feet are not yet set before she is screaming in his face, "How did you manage to become such a disgraceful human being, Kenneth?"

She can't keep her mouth and chin from twitching. Her left hand comes up reflexively to hide her face, but she redirects it to her shoulder as she turns away from him, coughing to suppress a sob.

"Is this about Lesser?"

She is not sure what he means, what he knows.

"So, this *is* about Lesser," he says.

"Ned."

"What does that mean, *Ned*?"

"It means Ned your brother-in-law was taken to the hospital in an ambulance."

"Oh yeah? What about Kitty?"

"I don't know."

"What do you mean you don't know?"

"I don't know anything."

"Did you call her?"

"I called the club."

"The club... So who were you talking to?"

"What?"

"Who was it you were talking to?"

"I don't know, some man at the front desk."

"You're not understanding, who were you talking to *in there*?" he says jabbing a finger at the pub.

"I don't know."

"You don't know?"

"Yes, I don't know. Now please."

"So Lesser was taken to the hospital? Huh."

"Oh God."

"What *oh God*? You know, I shouldn't say this but—"

"Just please shut up!"

"Okay, easy does it, Norma, easy does it. That's it, take a breath, good, that's right, that's right."

God help me, dear God, soon, soon.

"Look, I've known Ned a long time, longer than you. Love the guy, great guy, but... You see, I've been thinking a lot about Ned's celebrated epiphany. I've got this theory. Ned has a lot in common with those do-it-yourself visionaries. You know who I mean. The suburban loonies who see the Virgin Mary and Jesus in every piece of toast. I'm wagering Ned saw God at the bottom of a shot glass, got himself some Jesus, as they say. Let's not kid ourselves, Norma.

"So a couple of days ago I have what you could call a prophetic dream about good old Ned. He's jogging through a forest at one in the morning flapping his arms wanting to fly, but all he can manage is to hop up a couple of feet at a time, like a chicken. He's chasing after God, you see. I can read his thoughts being that it's a dream. I'm really concerned, so I start shouting, 'Ned, watch out for the trees! The trees, Ned! Watch out!'

"But the poor bastard is so loaded he can't hear me and hops up and slams right smack into a big old oak, breaks his nose and gashes up his face. There's blood all over his nice white shirt. From his broken nose. Because he ran into a tree. Because he was drunk as a skunk. Okay? So please, I'm begging you, Norma, can we put this chicken-shit gloom and doom crazy talk to rest now?"

"That's very amusing, Kenneth. You're right, you know Ned better than anyone and there's nothing to worry about. There never is with you."

She twists away and begins walking back to the pub.

"Thank you for agreeing, and where the hell are you going?"

"Good Lord, you haven't a clue."

"Oh, right. I suppose *you* know Ned. Maybe *you* can tell me what happened to him. Is there something *you'd* like to tell me, Norma? Some special knowledge *you* might want to impart about *Ned*?"

She stops, but not for the reason he thinks. He follows her gaze to a slight young man standing beneath the pub's entrance awning. Mars licks his lips as he scrutinizes the stranger, who is lit up like a jack-o-lantern by the ground lights on either side of the entrance. He looks back toward the road at a passing car, rubs his jaw, turns to take another quick glance at the stranger, tries to smile but just can't.

"Take the keys. Wait in the car. Please. I'll go get directions to the hospital. Please, Norma, get in the car."

She is waiting for the stranger to do something, but he appears increasingly more prop than man. She is immobilized, hoping in vain for something to happen.

Finally, the absurdity of her situation compels her to take the car keys from Mars. She opens the passenger door and waits for Mars to enter the pub.

The stranger has disappeared. She gets in the car, starts it up, turns the AC on low and reclines her seat. Almost immediately, she hears tapping on the window and sees the stranger hovering before her like an apparition.

"Go away," she says.

He makes a rolling motion with one hand, a descending motion with the other. She imagines him dressed like a harlequin performing pantomime at children's birthday parties to supplement his income.

"Go away."

He shakes his head no and smiles, a nice smile that transforms his face. He motions again for her to lower the car window. She obeys, watches the window slide down past his strangely pleasant smiling face.

"Please go, I will call you. I have your card."

The words sound strange coming out of her mouth. She doesn't like to lie. She has no intention of calling him and is fully aware he knows she is lying.

"Say my name," he says. "What does it cost you to say my name?"

"Werther Maria."

He looks at her with affection, and the unsolicited intimacy makes her look away, toward the pub entrance.

"You remembered my name, now you must tell me your name," he says. "Tell me your name. It is only right."

How many times had he played this tedious game with other women in this same dreary lot?

"Please."

"Venere," she says in her best Italian, her gaze fixed on the pub's entrance.

"Veh-neh-reh," he replies with eyes closed.

"Now go."

"Go? But you are too lovely."

A frail little sigh escapes her, one that had been fluttering inside her belly from the first moment he gazed at her. But she is not so naïve, she reminds herself, not so easily controlled, not some delicate flower whose petals are easily peeled.

And yet, there is a smile somewhere inside her to match his. Who could have told her that at her age she would crave such fleeting attentions? That words spoken to her by a complete stranger who referred to himself as Werther Maria Heilbronn would make her feel valued? But she cannot do this, she must not.

Did this man know her? Could he see the once glowing heart now long covered by the grime of time and heartbreak?

That he would look at her and form this thought of her, that he would say such words as he said. It makes her feel as happy as a new bride. To receive this one small mindless joy so unexpectedly at such a time in her life...

What does she care if it is a lie having already tasted its sweetness? What should her happiness or how she chooses to see things matter to anyone but her?

She feels as light as air in her newly created world. She tilts her head when he touches her neck, as if all along she had been anticipating this fresh mercy, this incarnation of pretty words. His fingers touch her skin like five kisses. She closes her eyes unencumbered by thought, and the vibrating thrum of the cicadas is no longer without, but within, stirring long dormant roots. She rests awhile in his vanishing whispers, *Venere, Venere*, and then opens her eyes.

Norma rubs her neck as she watches Mars approach, a plodding emblem of degeneracy.

He is waving a folded, scribbled-on menu sheet in feeble triumph. He raises his free hand. "Everything's going to be all right," he says, forcing a smile, but his words are like dust in the wind.

MARS AND NORMA go for a night ride, enduring the dim road's pessimistic commentary, managing fragments of memory and regret.

"Everything's going to be fine," Mars says with a thick throat as they get out of the car.

In minutes they are gazing down a hospital hallway at Kitty, who for a moment seems to be playing pat-a-cake with a young doctor. Riding the darkness, they had imagined the tincture of death seeping into the woman-child's porcelain white world, but neither is prepared for Kitty's grief-sharpened howl. A grim-faced nurse arrives on the scene, followed by a male orderly pushing a wheelchair.

Norma moves in a halting progression, as if measuring and re-measuring her steps. It occurs to her that maybe I was already dead when she waved goodbye to her sister-in-law. She quickens her pace.

Oh, the ugliness of her soul! (Her assessment, not mine.)

"Oh God, Kitty! I am so sorry!"

But Kitty doesn't know her. Norma staggers back, as if having been struck in the face. She twists her ankle and stumbles against Mars who catches her before she falls. Kitty lets out a piercing cry, "Kenny!"

They all defer to Mars, of course, but Kenny is awkward and unsure of himself as he holds in his arms the little woman with the buckling knees. Norma hobbles back down the hallway, her hand tapping the wall as she goes.

With all that is happening no one has noticed the stranger who has been standing by the elevator. Norma is not surprised to see him. The elevator swallows her and the stranger who follows her in.

"What floor?" she asks, and looks into his gray eyes that appear fixed on some unhappy dream.

"You are deranged, aren't you? A pathetic little man. But you can't see it, can you? No, it would be impossible for someone like you to see yourself the way others see you. Good Lord, what was I thinking? What do you want?"

He takes a deep breath, but can only stare at her.

"What do you want from me?" she says as the elevator doors close.

His hands are as ambivalent as his expression, moving first as if to cover his face, then to prepare the way for words. But the words die in his mouth.

"What is her name?" she says.

He looks to the side, then up, shakes his head, and attempts a smile.

"What is her name?" she insists.

"Carlotta."

Norma lunges at him, knocking him back against the elevator wall. She swings and lands several blows on his unprotected head, and just as abruptly she backs off, frowning at her fists, startled by her reaction. The stranger is dazed and pinned against the wall. He hides his eyes behind his hand.

"What do you want?"

She speaks gently now, in the way the suffering brave speak to one another, in hope-inflected tones. She studies his face and steps toward him, caresses his cheek and wipes his tears with her fingertips.

Then she places her head against his chest and listens to his heart.

His hand—light as that of a child—touches her bare arm. He holds her as if she were made of sculpted glass and whispers, "Oh, Venere, Venere."

She nudges him away. "Then take her away from him."

He pulls on his earring and shakes his head.

After a long pause he smiles like someone long resigned to misery. "Oh, I cannot, Venere, she is my brother's wife."

Of course, she is. Venere smiles. All she can think to do is kiss him on the lips, lightly, the way a mother might kiss her baby. She reaches for the button panel and the elevator doors slide open.

The young man's demeanor changes. He is neither alarmed nor intimidated by Mars's sudden presence.

With only the slightest hesitation, Venere takes Werther Maria's hand and kisses it, pats his cheek and steps out of the elevator.

"What are you going to do, Kenneth?" she says.

The question lingers on the border of his consciousness while he stares at the stranger, only half-believing such a creature can exist.

He looks away, up the hallway, fragments of the unfathomable whirling in his head: epiphanies, strangers, death. The intermittent glitter of the man's earring teases him with the possibility of significance to be gleaned, but all meaning and understanding elude him.

"Kitty's kids," she says. "Who's going to tell them their father is dead?"

The stranger's hand rises as if to elucidate but then vanishes. Mars watches the elevator doors slide shut and gazes at the seamed stainless-steel surface. He turns toward her and opens his mouth to speak but can only issue a piteous grunt. She studies the swollen lower lip and baggy eyes.

Her scrutiny weighs on him, coaxing from him three words. "Kitty, my God," he says, pointing meekly up the hallway.

No, that is not enough, not nearly enough.

"Who am I, Kenneth?"

His face contorts in disbelief.

"Kenneth, look at me. LOOK AT ME. Who am I?"

The words are strange and feel like a heavy weight being forced upon him.

But he is not stupid. This is all something of a shock, of course, the timing and confluence of things, the suddenness of it all, the massive impact of it all hitting him at once, too many things at once, just too many.

Who are you? You are asking me who you are?

Oh sure, he'd had inklings, foreshadowings, dreams, maybe even hallucinations, but *this*? What the hell was *this* exactly?

Was this hell?

A sudden rush of panic, eyes darting about, then mercy in the guise of a yield-to-no-horseshit moment. Close your eyes, Kenny, concentrate on Danny bringing home another King Arthur and keep thinking laughter is the best medicine, keep thinking sitting at home, swiveling. Let the smiles begin, let the laughter shine in—

Who *are* you?

Mars, Mars, is there no place for you in the new beginning? No clause for such as you written in the new terms and conditions?

Already he's forgotten Kitty, the kids, the reason he is standing in a hospital hallway, the reason Kitty is on the brink of tumbling into the abyss. Because too much thinking can flip you upside down, turn you inside out, poke you with the tip of the fear spear.

Mars hears voices flowing round the corner and down the corridor, an avalanche of tangled words that stir his tongue to a state of pre-enunciation. Something cogent wants saying, King Arthur notwithstanding, but darn if his tongue isn't on fire.

Mars, Mars. Is there no place for you?

Kenny, show the woman you too feel stirrings of newness. Show her you're up to the task, Kenny, go on.

But the burning tongue stiffens and crumbles to ash, the task of forging a new vocabulary for new thinking currently too big for Mars.

I don't really know who you are.

"Norma, you're Norma," he says like a child roused from a tricky dream.

A shadow of astonishment passes over her face. She turns her head and sees the orderly marching toward them.

The young man is frowning. He seems to want to say, *What is the problem? Why are you still standing there?*

"She has a simple heart," Venere explains.

The orderly stops before her, his African face a vexed and baffled tableau.

"Come with me, please," he says.

"Norma," Mars says.

"A simple heart is hard to find," Venere says.

"Norma!"

Mars watches the orderly and the woman move quickly up the corridor, turn right and disappear. He rubs his eyes with feverish intensity, takes a breath, and goes where he doesn't want to go.

Helen's Pendant

I'M LATE TO THE WAKE by design, sitting in my car. Should I stay or should I go?

I walk in real slow. First thing is Lyle receding into a wall. Taller than the last time I saw him, tall like his dad the roofer who's leading the two women away, the new wife and Helen's sister.

The casket's closed. I nod to the boy, who ignores me, nod to the women who stop and stare, nod to Callahan, who looks put out by my last second presence.

"My condolences," I say three times, once to each, like a rote penance.

The new wife nods in self-defense. Helen's sister is trying to understand my eyes, the Helen-Brian mystery. What can I tell her? I could say there is no explaining it. But how do I do that?

I don't.

They wait for me. I kneel before the casket, hear Callahan and the women whispering, feel Lyle being pulled out to sea, hear my heart tearing down the middle like cheap fabric.

Helen?

I place my hand on the casket, reconsider, remove it because of Lyle.

I would have died for you.

Whispers, oh, the damn whispers.

ON MY WAY TO WORK I stop at Helen's cubicle in Building 612.

Lyle's picture is gone, ladybug coffee mug I got her, gone, Sistine Chapel calendar she never explained where she got or why, gone. Jellybean jar, dogeared paperbacks, squeeze ball, stir-fry recipe book, all gone. Only the phone remains, old school, smug and squat as a ceramic Buddha.

A week later Morp calls me into his office.

"How are you, Brian?"

I check my watch.

"Right... Look, Brian, it goes without saying. Everybody, *everyone*, was devastated. It was the worst day ever. We all miss her beautiful smile, that way of hers... Tragically, and that's not even an adequate word for it, but is there an adequate word? I don't think so. *Tragically*, she's no longer with us. Helen is no longer with us, no. But yes, in a sense she is. Because in spirit yes, always, but physically, no. But you, Brian, you are with us spiritually *and* physically. Talk to me, bud."

Morp's smile is laced with crafted patience and understanding, life skills downloaded from his favorite life coach blog.

"Damn it, Brian, you've erected a wall around yourself, don't you see? It's been how many months? Whatever, a long time is my point, coming on a year. What I'm trying to tell you, son, is that it's time. It is time to knock down that wall. Help *me* help *you*. Let's knock it down together. Let's get you back on your feet!"

My face is a stone. Morp grimaces, realizing he needs to tone it down. He shakes his head, unhappy with the way that all came out.

"Good Lord, Brian," he says in just above a whisper. "I cannot imagine what is going on inside your head. Damn it, even now to think about it in any kind of focused way..."

"Hell, *that* is the problem, thinking too much, too deeply. I swear to you, sometimes I obsess about, you know, *The End*. The unglamorous grinding leadup to it, what it will be like for me, Jacqueline, the kids, the family. Sometimes I think I would rather get blindsided, squashed like a cockroach not knowing what hit me. Maybe that would be better.

"But in the meantime, Brian, what the hell are we supposed to do? We have to do something, right? So we work. The good thing about work is you do it with purpose and it can be therapeutic and fulfilling, not to mention profitable. You are a bright young man, Brian, one of our very best and right at the top of the Colonel's list. You know you are, and you know what they say, to whom much is given... Let me put it this way, the team depends on your leadership and expertise. They need *you* to help *them* produce the highest quality deliverable on a consistent basis."

"Of course," I say slapping my forehead. "Stupid small-minded me, forgetting the team and the high-quality deliverable."

"Come on, Brian, that's not fair. It was a matter of giving you space, people respecting your grief, maybe even being a little intimidated by it. You have to understand, you got a little scary there for a while, son. I don't mean to—"

"All right, Nelson, all right. I get it. I'll be less scary."

I get up, turn to leave, but Morp isn't finished.

He stands up and, still not satisfied with how our little conversation has gone, summons his Deputy Program Manager voice: "Not only do we strive, as a *team*, Brian, to give the warfighter the highest quality deliverable on a *consistent* basis, but to do so in the most *expeditious* manner."

Oh, Morp is right, of course, but what he said notwithstanding I'm having trouble suppressing a desire to punch him in the face, launch a quick nose-mouth jab, a shock and awe strike. I step toward him, my right shoulder in mid-roll. He shrinks back, his face contorting. I stop and take a breath.

"I need to breathe, Nelson. Right now, I'm just really needing to breathe. I'm taking the rest of the day off."

Morp clears his throat. "Good idea, Brian. Take the rest of the day. We can talk tomorrow."

I WALK OVER TO BUILDING 612. First time in a week. Helen's abandoned desk is a shrine to me, a dread spot to others, like a house where a murder has been committed.

No one goes near the desk, or me. They know how ungracious I can be. And how scary.

Sitting in Helen's chair, looking at the flat bare surface where her things used to be, I pick up her telephone receiver, hold it to my mouth, press my lips into the tiny holes that drank her voice how many times? Run my fingertips over the blocky keypad, absorb Helen oils, rub her into my eyelids, top and bottom, rub her like an ointment to help me see beyond these here-now walls. I see the moon beach hair loose and wild in the wind, and Helen's uplifted arms charming the captive stars.

When I put the receiver back in its cradle, I notice something poking out from beneath the base of the telephone unit, like the tip of a red tongue. I nudge the unit back to reveal a magic marker valentine. Inside, *Helen loves Brian*.

Damn, Helen...

Helen, like a kid after her first kiss.

An arrow punctures the middle of the heart and pokes out the other side. Three drops of blood leap in the air like happy sweat off a cartoon face. I touch each drop with the tip of my finger. This one. This one. This one.

Not cute, not funny.

I cover my nose and mouth, press the side of my face against her desk that is smoothed by years of hands and elbows and arms and scented of maple, of goodness, of Helen.

If I break...

Breathe, Brian, breathe.

If I break now...

If I break now, it won't matter because I don't care about spectacle gossip pity recriminations. I don't care about—

Who touched my shoulder?

Helen?

Is it you?

Holly? What are you doing?

Run, Holly! Run, you poor girl, run.

AN AWAKENING? A new way of seeing? Something changed the moment Holly Perez touched my shoulder.

I don't know how to explain it, but I know I can't stay. I'm leaving on a jet plane, as the song goes. No more Fort Chance for me, no more Morp, no more ghosts. Yesterday marked a personal milestone because I smiled while thinking of Helen, first time since the moonlit sea stole her from me.

Holly is wonderful, like a dose of cherry-flavored medicine. I won't let her get too close, though. Wouldn't be right. One day she shows up wearing a cross pendant exactly like the one Helen was wearing our last night together. Throws me for a loop, puts me in a bad place.

What the hell is this? I'm thinking. A sign? A sign of what? But it passes. I try to let it go. Holly is wonderful, sweet, and pretty as honey, but she's not Helen.

I can talk to her about Helen, but not too much I realize soon enough. She tells me about old boyfriends and why she never married, and it all makes sense to me. She says she likes being independent. That's good, I say, but also good to go out with guys now and then, give yourself the opportunity to find someone you can connect with in a meaningful way. When I start talking this way, she gets quiet and I know it's time to say goodnight.

AFTER MUCH DELIBERATION, I make a phone call. Lyle's stepmother informs me she will let Lyle's father know I called and will get back to me. Even as I say goodbye, I am regretting having made the call.

For days I can think of nothing else. After all these months, out of the blue, I call the Callahans? They must have thought me unhinged.

But one day my phone rings. The new Mrs. Callahan sounds a bit unsteady, a tad ambivalent. Regrettably, she cannot give me Lyle's phone number, but she can give me his P.O. Box address at RU.

"Mr. Callahan, uh, Mr. Callahan and I, we were thinking about Lyle's welfare, okay, *that* above all else, and taking everything into account, like how talking with you might, uh, you know, thirteen months removed... A brief note, though. That would be fine, I think. A brief note if you would like to send him one. That would be fine with us."

"You've been very helpful," I say, "and I hope one day—"

I stop in midsentence, my attention diverted by the sound of ice cubes colliding in a glass. I can smell the alcohol on her breath from half a state away. I thank her for the P.O. Box address and hang up the phone.

BEFORE DAWN at the kitchen table with several sheets of printer paper and holding in my hand the silver pen Helen gave me on Valentine's Day. I'm thinking of her and her only child and what I want to say.

I approach the task from a couple of different angles, tear up the sheets, start again, settle on the following:

Hey Lyle,

We never got to talk much. I'm sorry about that. Maybe someday—I hope someday—that will change. I hope you're adjusting to college life okay. Good to have that first month under your belt. I have to tell you, for me that first semester at RU—yes, I went there too—was a lesson in humility. Maybe it won't be so bad for you. I sense you're smarter than me.

I'll be moving to New Mexico in a few days. If you ever want to talk about anything, or need a place to crash if you're in the area. You call me any time you want, Lyle, day or night, for any reason. I know you have my cell phone number. Your Mom told me she put it in your phone in case you ever had to, you know, contact me for whatever reason.

Lyle, I went through a really bad phase in my life a while back. I got diverted, couldn't see straight, couldn't make good decisions. I told your Mom we needed time apart. It took me some time before I realized I couldn't live without her. She took me back and we were happy and then everything changed so suddenly...

I can't tell you I understand why things happen. I have no clue. Some people say everything happens for a reason. I don't know. Seems an easy thing to say. Too neat for me, I guess. Others say you're better off not believing in anything. I'm somewhere in between, I guess, trying to sort things out, trying to figure out what's true and maybe what's not.

But you know something, Lyle, one thing I know for sure is true, and that's thanks to your Mom: Love is the truest thing. That may sound corny, but when everything else goes away, love stays. You just have to remember it's there. It's always there. But you have to be open to it. You have to have eyes to see it, and a heart to embrace it. I think you already know that because you're Helen's son.

I was a fool. I allowed vanity and cheap thrills to govern my life and keep me from being open to the real deal. But I'm done with all that. Don't go where I went, Lyle.

Take care, buddy, and know that your Mom loved you with the strength of angels.

Brian Mares

OVER COFFEE AND DESSERT, Brian tells me his plan. He can't keep from glancing at the pendant hanging from my neck while we talk, and I try not to notice or be uncomfortable about it.

I can smile and nod only so much because of what he's telling me and because the second thing that popped into my head when I heard Helen died was that after she was gone awhile, he would want me because of the electricity that happened when he touched my hand the day we were introduced.

The first thing was the act of God. That was the first thing I thought when I heard she died, that it was caused by an act of God, and that led to the second thing, about how that act of God could mean something special for Brian and me and our future together because of the electricity that flowed between us when we met, like we were flowing one into the other.

I'm prettier than Helen (than she *was*), and younger. He can see that. He knows it. Everybody could tell you the same thing. I can give him beautiful sons and daughters, his very own, as many as he wants.

I'm trying to understand it all, the act of God and why Brian wants to go away and leave a great job to work as a bus driver.

I try to imagine the vistas he describes to me, his eyes far away when he talks like that. *The stark shadows and brilliant hues.* God help me. I pretend to understand this *resurrected childhood zeal* for painting he keeps talking about.

Should I tell him how I feel about him? But he already knows, it makes no difference.

He wants to go away, be a bus driver, paint pictures.

Better he leave now. From the start my role in his life was destined to be limited, despite the act of God. I can see that now. We're too different, and I don't know the first thing about *stark shadows and brilliant hues* or whatever artist or writer *gets it,* like he says.

Gets what?

I know what I feel when I'm near him. I remember his hand touching mine, the electricity, and how I couldn't sleep that night until I put my hand down there. And then came the terrible day my hand burned when I touched his shoulder.

I wanted him to know me, but I got scared and ran away. Did that quicken his day of decision? Maybe I wasn't a factor at all. Maybe I think myself too important. Or he just doesn't love me, period, and maybe never could, though if he just gave me the chance...

Oh, merciful God, help me, forgive me. I confessed touching myself. The old priest waited patiently for more sins. When I confessed my brief joy at Helen's death, I heard him sigh. I felt the need to elaborate. It was a reflex, I said, something I didn't mean to happen. A horrible unforgivable reflex.

But yours is a contrite heart, he assured me. God loves a contrite heart, forgives a contrite heart. We all fall short. We all are sinners.

Then why is this contrite heart still an anguished heart?

I talked to Helen last night. She was floating above my bed, staring at me. She said nothing. I think she is angry because of the pendant.

I make myself cheer up and tell Brian how I am learning to play the guitar, how I plan to visit Paris in the spring with a couple of girls from the office. But he cannot get it out of his mind. It is eating him up. I run out of things to say.

He points to it. "Is that new?" he says.

"I found it," I tell him. "I was walking barefoot on the beach last summer and the chain looped itself around my big toe and came up

125

out of the sand. I placed it in my jewelry box and kept it there. I almost forgot I had it. One day I happened to notice it, picked it up and put it on. Don't you like it?"

Why did I say that? Why would I say such a thing?

I wait for Brian to respond but he's far away again, somewhere deep inside his coffee cup.

"Brian, are you okay?"

He glances up at me. "Yeah, I'm fine, Holly. Sorry, I was just remembering something."

I do *get it,* not all of it, but enough to understand his need to move on, or at least I try to understand.

So I tell him Mrs. Mackey has informed me they will be getting a new receptionist to take my place after the holidays. They are going to start training me so I can begin working in Nicole's group. He looks concerned and I imagine he is thinking they will put me in his beloved Helen's old desk.

I am not worthy, I am not worthy, I am so not worthy. I think I am going to cry. I cannot cry. I cannot run.

Oh, merciful God, help me.

I go back to church and confess lying to Brian about the pendant. I tell the priest I saw it by chance one day in the mall and decided to purchase it because it was the exact same pendant Helen used to wear. The old priest waits patiently as I try to explain, but I go on too long. I know I have totally confused him. When I grow quiet, he says God loves a contrite heart, forgives a contrite heart. We all fall short. We all are sinners.

WHENEVER THE WIND IS STRONG, I think of Helen, her wild hair and moonlit curves, the jealous sea. And then I think of Lyle. He never got back to me. I wonder what he thought of my letter. I think he may have rolled his eyes as he showed it to his roommate. I think he may have said, what a douchebag.

The farewell party is very nice, really special, and so greatly appreciated I tell those who dare ask. Nicole and Morp honor me with brief, clever speeches. At the end there are hugs, some implied, and oodles of kisses, the errant tear wiped away with discretion. No one wants to remember what happened all those months ago. Holly is subdued and detached.

On behalf of the BMD folks, Nicole presents me a tin bucket filled with tubes of oil paints and a mix of hog bristle and sable bristle brushes with red white and blue bows fixed to the bucket handle. Morp has his longtime admin, Linda Norris, who will be retiring before Christmas, present me with a leather satchel on behalf of all the TMD people.

Alexa Forster (née Adwell) chooses not to attend. Our Budget Analyst's absence comes as no surprise to me or anyone else. Alexa and I had an arduous fling. I was relieved when I heard she was getting married. The lucky fellow is Marlon "Rock" Forster, a retired Lieutenant Colonel at Fort Chance and current CEO of an Information Services company. I imagine Alexa sees Helen's death as a sign of God's wrath.

The final week at the Fort passes quickly. No one expects me to attend every meeting and participate in every sidebar, but I feel a strong sense of obligation. Perhaps it is my way of atoning for past lapses, indiscretions, and random acts of scariness. When I'm not in meetings I'm organizing data, writing up reports, instructions and guidelines, leaving everything in perfect order for my successor who, as yet, remains TBD.

When the time comes, I don't want to see anyone. I wait until lunchtime on a Friday, a period of routinely high attrition. I send off a brief parting email to my team and a few individual *thank you* notes that I prepared beforehand. I shut down and unplug my laptop. I tap my desk farewell, leave the door to my office wide open, and start heading with my laptop to IT and Security to get out-processed.

On my way I stop at Morp's office to say goodbye. He is my mentor, after all. Morp likes to work through lunch on Fridays so he can get a head start on the weekend. But Morp is not there. I walk into the Men's Room, but no Morp there either. I think of all the times Helen hid from me when I would show up in Building 612 after breaking up with her. I wonder if Morp is also hiding from me, but I decide that would just be too strange.

Outside, I dally on the steps of Building 610. I stare a long while across the way at Building 612 imagining the restless shadows inside bandying about and checking their watches.

The impulse is so strong I almost cry out for help: Damn it, Helen... I know you don't want me going back in there. You know I can't.

I reach in my coat, slip my hand inside my shirt and feel the cross pendant with my fingertips. I feel the up and down of it, the left and right of it, the all-around of it.

Last night Holly took it off her neck and placed it around mine. I resisted halfheartedly, said no, it would not look right on me.

"But it's a gift," she said with a most righteous look on her face, "and it would be wrong for you to say no."

Everybody Needs Closure

THE PROSPECT OF SPYING on Orson Massey left me feeling dirty and irritated and anxious to get my life back on track. But for some time, I had been making an effort to keep all things in perspective.

I reminded myself that walking out of Building 610 was a good in and of itself and that just six workdays separated me from my long-desired new beginning.

Across the big cold parking lot I went, bearing the scrutiny of row upon row of impenetrable windshields. Behind the random glare, I knew more than one poor slob was stealing ten or fifteen minutes of down time.

I wasn't going to put any one of them on the spot by stopping to stare, like Harvey the logistician liked to do. Not that I was better than Harvey. I wasn't. But I did understand the need to get away as much as anyone.

The old balding Corolla started right up and I could see from where I sat that Orson was just then buckling his seat belt. Had he been entertaining second thoughts?

Orson liked to park as far away from Building 610 as possible, in an otherwise empty lot that extended off the main Command parking lot like a narrow peninsula.

"Walking trumps caffeine," my hefty colleague liked to say, but I had long ago recognized in this habit the workings of a fastidious and jealous nature.

The pristine Cadillac DeVille shared an air of *Look but don't touch* with the local strippers, those voluptuous ballerinas who pole-danced at *The Fox Hole*, the place to which, I suspected, Orson was heading.

I followed the champagne-colored DeVille off Post onto the gray county road thinking how you could never predict how people would react to change. Every couple of years the Base Realignment and Closure rumors would resurface, but no one paid them much serious attention until one day BRAC turned into a legitimate rampaging multiheaded monster, a socioeconomic hydra that went about wreaking havoc on family life, housing, careers, retirement plans, and local commerce.

The decision to shut down Fort Chance came at a very bad time, not that there could be a good time. The two-year transition of resources and operations two hundred miles to the south—still only in its first six months—had produced attrition among the workforce and a grinding down of the esprit de corps expected of civilian employees of the US Army.

BRAC in itself failed to unhinge me. On the contrary, it served as the impetus for my decision to start a new life. Unfortunately, the same could not be said for many of my colleagues.

Was BRAC the reason Orson sighed so often? I didn't know the answer to that question, nor did I care. Some things just weren't all that important to me. But I had made a promise to Mrs. Massey, and it was essential that I keep my word, if only to have one less reason to hate myself.

I thought about Orson's wife and what she had sounded like on the phone and how I had felt embarrassed for her, as one might when the person talking to you is completely lacking in self-awareness or has reached an emotional point of no return. Maybe Mrs. Massey was just your run of the mill drama queen, and maybe her husband was one too.

It did seem to me that if having a drink at a strip club to relieve BRAC-induced stress was the worst thing Orson could be accused of, Mrs. Massey should consider herself lucky.

It was not all that difficult to figure out why Orson might lie to his wife. Mrs. Massey could be as ingenuous and sweet as a preschooler, but her high-pitched voice and indefatigable tongue could bring a man to his knees. From an objective standpoint, I could argue that Orson's strategy to evade rather than to engage was sound, but I also understood that Orson's growing conjugal aloofness was what got me dragged into this marital quagmire, and frankly, I could do without the surplus drama. There was already enough drama to wrestle with in my own head to have to grapple with someone else's.

Still, there was no point in heaping misery upon misery. I kept reminding myself to approach the task at hand as a kind of diversion, though I was not totally indifferent to Mrs. Massey's concerns.

Was Orson capable of slipping a twenty in a stripper's thong? Maybe, though I doubted it. Orson was a miser. But I could visualize the big man slouched in a dark corner of the strip club curling his handlebar mustache while ogling the topless dancers from a safe distance, possibly even slinking off to a stall in the Men's Room at some point to culminate his fantasy. And maybe that was enough reason for a wife to worry.

To my surprise, however, the DeVille rolled right past *The Fox Hole* without the slightest hesitation. I watched the weedy gravel lot and windowless chocolate-colored structure recede in my rearview mirror. I felt a stab of disappointment and immediately recognized its source. As much as I hated to admit it, since I had agreed to Mrs.

Massey's request to keep tabs on her husband, *The Fox Hole's* dim fleshy interior had hovered before me like a fantastic oasis, despite my one unfortunate incident there days after Jenny's death.

After several miles we were driving through what passed for a town center with its handful of small, decorated lit-up storefronts that lured last minute shoppers with their colorful displays of gadgets and bric-a-brac.

This had been Jenny's favorite time of year. Last December at the PM-CNOPS Christmas party she had walked up to me. "I'm betting you'd rather be anywhere but here," she had said with a big smile.

Those were the first words she spoke to me.

Two weeks later we were in each other's arms in Times Square kissing as the New Year's ball was descending and the great shout was going up. She was drunk and chatty, and I was drunk and confused.

"Isn't it great, David?" she kept saying. "Isn't it all going to be so wonderfully great?" And I'd said "Yes, yes," and that was all I could remember from that night.

I flipped open my wallet as I drove and glanced at my favorite picture of Jenny, that big smile of hers and the lively green eyes and shiny brown hair pulled back into a neat bun. I always knew it was a mistake to pull out that picture, but I did it anyway as a kind of self-flagellation.

I thought about Santa Cruz de Tenerife where I would soon be. A thin sidewalk Santa jingled her bell with a tired arm and soon the specialty shops were giving way to gas stations and convenience stores.

A short while later Orson peeled off the main drag. I followed at what I deemed a prudent distance through a wasteland of abandoned lots, boarded-up buildings, old warehouses and a crumbling brick factory. Finally, we entered a residential area of one-way streets and row houses with jutting stoops that triggered childhood memories of plastic-covered couches, peeling wall paint, and the stink of cockroach insecticide.

I was lagging a half block behind when Orson came to a complete stop. I glided the Corolla to the opposite curb to get a better view of Orson, and pulled up behind a rusted old Buick laid out on four flat tires. Orson took his time aligning the DeVille against the curb, then got out and stared at the brick building. He appeared to be mulling over the potential ramifications of what he was about to do.

Standing there on the sidewalk in his big tan overcoat, black-rimmed glasses, and handlebar mustache, Orson seemed as out of place as a bear. He labored up the concrete steps and rang the doorbell.

After a short delay a woman stuck her head out of a second-floor window and tossed a key that bounced off Orson's hand onto the sidewalk. Orson retrieved the key and climbed back up the steps and disappeared into the building.

It was nearly four o'clock, overcast and raw with night fast approaching. I drove slowly past 139 South Street and circled the block before parking behind a dirty white van about fifty yards from the DeVille.

My breath rose in damp puffs as I walked toward the apartment building, not sure what I intended to do. I recalled a forecast of snow for later in the day as I climbed the steps. The locked door felt thick and heavy. I peered through the hazy napkin-sized door window at mud-colored stairs. A shabby brown banister rose toward some peculiar forum of infidelity.

I glanced up and down the street and, perhaps prompted by some vague memory of Sherlock Holmes, I stooped to sniff the doorknob as though seeking an odor of revelation. It was an unfortunate pose that did not escape the notice of two small boys who startled me with sharp jabs of laughter. They poked their noses at the air like trained seals and stuck out their rear ends in extravagantly cruel pantomime.

An idea came to me. I stepped toward the boys in a conciliatory way, but they weren't buying it. They dashed off to a safe distance from which to observe me. Their small sinewy bodies resumed the savage mockery that so amused them.

"Hey guys, who's the lady that lives up on the second floor?" I said.

The boys stopped their gyrations and stared at me. The smaller of the two jammed both thumbs into his nostrils and gazed at me mournfully.

"I'm playing a prank on an old friend," I said. "I'll give you ten dollars if you ring the top doorbell. I'll be across the street hiding under the stoop in that building over there. All you have to do is ring the top doorbell, and you get to keep the ten dollars."

The boys argued briefly before the larger one said, "What you waitin' for? We ain't got all day."

I stretched a ten in the air between my fingers to show I meant business and wedged the bill under the door. I crossed the street, turned, smiled and gave them the thumbs-up sign. They both responded with a thumbs-down and pretended to defecate.

What should I have expected?

The larger boy hopped up the steps like a sandpiper and plucked the ten-dollar bill. The youngster flashed me a big roguish smile and, to my amazement, lunged at the top button and pressed it for a legitimate three-count before scampering down the steps.

I hid by the entrance of the cellar tunnel across the street. The second-floor window opened with a languid woody moan. I was stunned when Marjorie Carlsen's big pink face emerged out of the brick wall.

The softspoken cleaning girl glanced at the steps below for an instant then turned to watch the pranksters dashing down the middle of the street. She watched them disappear.

She had always seemed to me the type of person who bore insult without protest, and I did not know if that was good or bad. She turned her head in my direction and scanned the vicinity as though expecting to find a more substantial and threatening entity than the two boys.

I ducked just in time and drew myself deeper into the damp, urine-scented space, sidestepping the label of a shattered vodka bottle. Gossamer webs covered all four corners of a door that looked as though it hadn't been opened in years.

Outside, the window groaned as Marjorie lowered it. What would I tell Mrs. Massey? Would I be prepared for the barrage of questions and frantic speculations? Might it be better to confront Orson directly? And what about Marjorie? Did I owe Marjorie some kind of heads-up?

It would have been a simple matter now to start up the car, turn on the heat and drive away. But the prospect of having to brief Mrs. Massey grew increasingly daunting. Marjorie's involvement added an unexpected twist to the matter and in some arcane way seemed to— in my mind at least—implicate *me*. The whole affair was annoyingly invasive. I really didn't need such complications at this juncture of my life.

After weighing my options, I decided to relieve myself of the burden of reporting back to Mrs. Massey. I would confront Orson directly and suggest to him that *he* talk to his wife. No doubt our exchange would get ugly.

Even so, it remained by far the lesser of two evils, and the prospect of soon never again having to deal with the Masseys cemented my decision.

I got into the Corolla and wondered how long a wait I could manage. It didn't take long for the cold to seep into my toes and fingers.

Starting up the car would draw attention, so I rubbed my hands and bounced my feet instead. In the midst of imagining the warm breezes of Tenerife, a small Asian woman appeared as if out of thin air. She paddled over the sidewalk carrying an enormous backpack.

The streetlights flickered on just as she glided past the Corolla and I imagined she was a sorceress.

About fifteen minutes later I spotted a gang of nearly a dozen predatory teens muscling their way down the center of the poorly lit street. They were boasting in profanities and shoving and taunting one another, each one louder than the next.

I feared they might begin to fight among themselves, or worse, make camp upon the DeVille and linger there. But they were too charged up to pause, and I was glad when they passed without taking notice of my slumped form.

I told myself I would wait until six for Orson, but not a minute longer. If no Orson, I'd stop at the mall, grab a couple of slices of pizza at the food court, cogitate awhile, then go home and watch TV until my eyelids dropped.

Or I could get a cheeseburger and beer at *The Fox Hole* and cogitate there...

Oh, that temptation was always near, tucked beneath a fold in my brain like a dirty little consolation prize. But this time would have to be different. I would stay in the back, keep my mouth shut, limit my consumption to one or maybe two drinks, no more.

This time—if there was this time—would it be different? While recovering from my post-Jenny concussion, I had cogitated long and hard and come up with one gleaming-like-a-diamond thought: *There are no limits to a man's stupidity.*

Initially, I wrote the words down in reference to myself. Reading them made me want to write them again, which I did, a total of three-hundred times.

One-hundred times for each time my head got bounced off the hood of the Corolla. At first, I wrote in silence, but soon I was reciting the words out loud. The repeated words had a soothing effect on me, the way I imagine repetitive prayer has a soothing effect on the pious.

Sitting in the cold car, staring at the dent in the hood where my head had thrice been bounced, I recited the mantra with a steady voice: "There are no limits to a man's stupidity. There are no limits to a man's stupidity. There are no limits to a man's stupidity."

If Orson failed to appear I would inform Mrs. Massey that I saw him enter 139 South Street in Chancetown. Any further details regarding his activity that Thursday afternoon should be provided to her by her husband, not me. That was my plan, but I really had no idea what I would do.

Were there any assurances about anything? In my life all good and worthy things had proved elusive, or at best fleeting, possessed for only the briefest time before slipping away. I had come to accept that a plan was merely a coping mechanism, an illusion of control, a means by which we are able to put one foot in front of the other. When had any plan of mine, on any significant level, panned out? The returns were not good, and I often wondered if life was just one big tease.

Mrs. Massey's awkward and moving note to me after Jenny died had kept me up for nights, its baroque, handwritten words echoing in my feverish brain like a psalm: *If you are patient enough, David, if you believe hard enough, pray hard enough, Jenny will come back to life.* Such words would make it impossible for me—nearly half a year later—to decline the desperate woman's strange request.

Of course, Jenny did not come back to life, but she did become like a warm liquid that circulated within me day and night, lifting to my brain the occasional suggestion and assurance. But gradually, those blood whispers began to fade and I knew it was time to make a new life for myself.

I was offered a job to head up the new Internet Sciences department at the *Instituto Politécnico* in Santa Cruz de Tenerife, Spain. At times the whole business seemed to me a trick of the mind. My successful interview there had the vague, receding feel of a dream, as did the brief phone call from Raul Ibarra, the department head, who informed me I was their first choice to fill the position—that is, if I wanted it.

I accepted immediately, before we could firm up any of the details, my impulsiveness eliciting hearty laughter from Mr. Ibarra. Or at least that was how I remembered our exchange.

My imminent move to Spain to begin my new life there seemed as contrived as bad fiction.

But I had the papers. The signed papers were proof something new did indeed await me. I touched and read those papers most evenings to help foster pleasant dreams. Dual citizenship, fluency in Spanish, appropriate technical experience and the absence of commitments all suited me well. Soon I would be far from the Masseys and anything that hinted of chaos and sorrow.

If only it were that easy to forget all things... The cool cloying sand, the briny wind and lusty waves, the coarse bright moon and laughing stars had all congregated that night. Jenny had laughed with great joy, had turned and dashed away, a flash of white against the black waters. "I love you, David," she had shouted. On our way there she told me she had lettered in swimming her sophomore, junior and senior years in high school.

I lay my head back against the car seat and closed my eyes. I focused on a point in the blazing darkness and moved toward it.

AT SIX-THIRTY SHARP the DeVille roared back to life, waking me from half sleep. I stared at Orson's car as it angled back toward the curb. I started up the Corolla and quickly swung it past the DeVille into the middle of the one-way street, blocking Orson's path. The big car continued to creep forward, tentatively—like a wary dog testing the limits of its master's resolve—before coming to a stop a car-length away.

The DeVille's headlights were in my eyes, preventing me from seeing Orson. Their projection highlighted the gravity of our impending clash. I imagined Orson immobilized by humiliation and, no doubt, simmering rage. As I drew near, I saw only shadows. I pressed my forehead against the driver side window and there he was, lying on his side like a slain buffalo, his face buried in the passenger seat.

I tapped on the window several times and waited, but the large man refused to move. I rapped my knuckles against the glass and whispered curses at the sky as Orson raised himself and adjusted his glasses and mustache.

Orson's expression of concern appeared reserved for the DeVille's mahogany dashboard, which was marred by an untoward speck that he removed with the tip of his right pinky.

I pounded the window with my open hand until I heard the curt assent of the released door locks. I walked around the front of the car, opened the passenger side door and stood in the threshold cultivating a long moment of passive aggression before climbing in.

A lovely piano composition whispered through the roar of the heating fan like a distant intimacy. I warmed myself while listening to the CD Orson had selected for the occasion.

"Chopin?" I said.

Orson ignored me and turned his head toward the driver side window. But there was no running away, no vanishing into thin air, no popping his unwieldy bulk through that narrow window into a reality of his choosing.

My patience waning, I reminded myself that the sole purpose of my sitting in that big warm car on a snow-threatened December work night was to get Orson to talk to his wife so I wouldn't have to.

I opened my mouth to speak, but Orson beat me to it.

"I know Morp sent you."

"Morp?"

"I know he did, there's no use denying it. I also know what you heard me say to that fiendish Belinda. Do you think me fool enough to risk my professional reputation by misrepresenting two measly hours on my time card?"

I could not quite decide if Orson was being serious or pulling my leg or whether I was witnessing the man's freefall into madness.

Orson stared back at me somewhat wild-eyed. I felt as though I had poked a sleeping bear.

"We all know her modus operandi," Orson continued, speaking with uncharacteristic vigor. "There is never any good reason to tell Belinda anything that might — or should I call her *Malinda*? — anything at all, in fact, that might set her fiendish little mind in motion, all instances of personal leave converted in her wicked brain into occasions of sin. Oh, we pagans, we reprobates, we incorrigibles. 'I'm going to a meeting,' I announce without warning as I walk away, and leave it at that, no explanations, no details."

Did Orson think me a fool?

I stared at his profile for several moments and then studied the little Corolla, so sad and vulnerable there in the middle of the poorly lit street. We sat in silence listening to a lovely nocturne and the spirited heating fan. I wasn't going anywhere.

Finally, seeing no way out, Orson grimaced in a protracted manner that appeared to necessitate medical intervention. He gripped the steering wheel and shook his head, arms and legs as he let out a prodigious groan.

"For misery's sake!" he shouted, dropping his hands to his thighs and turning his large head to glare at me.

"Would it have been such a burden for you to play along? Would it have killed you to say, 'Yes, Morp sent me to remind you to enter the correct charge code on your timecard'? Never mind the implausibility, the patent absurdity. That is irrelevant. With a wink and a nod, we could have called it a day and been on our way home with no regrets."

"Look, Orson, I don't care what you do or why you do it. It's none of my business. I'm only here because—"

"Because everything has changed. You could have spared us both, but you chose not to, and here we are. I ask myself, 'Why is this happening? Why do I now suddenly feel obligated to explain things to *him*?'"

"I don't need or want explanations. I don't need or want to understand anything. Talk to your wife. This is about you talking to your wife, nothing more."

Orson turned and stared at me with dead eyes. His head and body seemed to expand, claiming too much of our limited space. I felt the need for air.

"She has accused me of lying to her more than once, you know. When I dismissed her claim, she threatened to have you follow me... But why *you*? I wonder."

"I'm not the one you should ask."

Orson stared at me with those same dead eyes for a long time and then broke into hearty laughter.

"Women are full of surprises, are they not? She was afraid I would get into trouble at the strip club. Or so she told you. How rich. How rich, indeed. I recall an incident involving you some months ago..."

He laughed again. His laughter filled the car and buffeted me, roiling my thoughts and inducing the beginnings of a headache. Then he stopped laughing suddenly and turned off the heating fan. His tone became philosophic.

"We are left to wonder what goes on in a woman's mind. Why, for goodness' sake, would Paulina not tell you she suspected I was seeing someone? That instead she would have you believe you were on your way to a *girlie bar*, as she put it... I can explain."

"I'm not interested in your explanation."

"The sad truth, Pintor, is that for two years I was unable to perform sexually with Paulina. But we found ways to compensate. Meats, pastas, breads, and soups constituted an erotic language in and of themselves. Cakes, pies, truffles, etcetera. You have overheard us discuss what we had for dinner the night before, what we were looking forward to eating the evening to come, ideas for the following day and so on. To an obsessive degree? Perhaps. But understand, these meals became our subsidiary genitals, the means by which, for lack of alternatives, we pleasured one another. No urologist, no little blue tablet, no bushel of oysters was able to remedy what ailed me, Pintor, at least not with Paulina. For a very long time I believed my condition was irreversible..."

He looked at my bewildered face and said, "Let us clear the air, shall we? Marjorie Carlsen and I were friends long before you set foot in Building 610."

He paused again and stared at me. Expecting what? That I would throw myself off the Empire State Building? What did he want of me? Why was he telling me these things?

"Marjorie and I discovered that we could talk at length about many things. She is deceptively bright, despite what one might think given her innate reticence and that unflattering uniform she is made to wear. She is an exceptional young woman, but I must tell you something about her you will not like. She lied to you when she told you about Molly...

"If only you could see your face. It is not what you think. What she said about her little sister was true, and to this day the drowning haunts her. She was playing inside with a friend when it happened. She was nowhere near the pool. Where were the adults? Marjorie was not to blame, yet she told you it was her fault. And then she led you to believe you were the first one to hear her *confession*. But I was the one who knew the truth. I was the one who held her as she wept. I was the only one."

Orson gazed at me. His expression was clinical but tinted faintly of frustration. He removed his glasses and began to wipe the lenses with the wide end of his tie. His voice changed as he resumed. The words tumbled out of his mouth with slow, somber precision, like jurors walking out of a deliberation room.

"Marjorie thought lying to you an act of charity." He paused for effect, wiping the lenses slowly, methodically.

He took a deep breath and shook his head as if in disbelief before continuing.

"Her need to confess a sin that was not a sin had already, long before, found a compassionate and understanding listener in me. She suspected you blamed yourself for what happened to Jenny. She believed that revealing to you *her* sin—a sin that was, in fact, no sin at all—would help ease the guilt of your own."

Orson snuck a glance at me and returned to his lens cleaning.

"I have often wondered, Pintor. Did it work?"

I turned and stared at that loathsome profile. The complacent wiping of eyeglasses continued unabated. The man's girth suddenly became impossibly offensive to me. The fold of pink hair-spiked neck bulging over the white collar, the overused striped blue tie and overstretched black wingtips, the body mass that seemed to expand with each moment, robbing me of precious oxygen.

All that was Orson appeared designed and impelled to crush me. A sharp pain shot through the left side of my head as my hand squeezed itself into a tight fist.

There are no limits...

In a blur of anxious nausea, I struggled to complete the prayer that was not a prayer.

There are no limits to misery...

I clenched my jaw and felt my breaths grow fast and shallow.

Orson stopped what he was doing and stared solemnly at his lap. His breathing became quiet and steady. A mournful serenity began to exude from him and permeated the confined space of the DeVille's interior. A passerby might have thought Orson asleep or in a state of meditation.

He turned his head slowly toward me, as though his soul had grown weary. He was a different man now, a man stripped of all presumption, a man of different proportion and temperament, psychologically deflated. His eyeglasses dangled from his left hand. He gazed at me with myopic eyes.

"I have certain issues, Pintor. We all have our demons."

He tilted his head as if he were waiting to be kissed on the cheek.

"If it would help you... I promise I will not retaliate, nor hold it against you."

Orson shut his eyes and awaited the blow. The immense small-eyed face loomed oddly before me, as though suspended solely by the haunting notes of a nocturne.

The tension in my body began to dissipate. The ache in my head diminished. Orson opened his eyes and waited for me to say something, but I gave him no reason to think I wanted to. He put his glasses back on, pulled on the right side of his mustache, took a deep breath and continued.

"Very well, then, if I may. This does concern you, believe it or not. I shared with Marjorie my growing dissatisfaction with life. She listened without expression, without uttering a word. One day you arrived to the Command. I confess, I was quite disappointed to see Marjorie gravitate toward you. I tried to understand things from her perspective. I was married. I had nothing to offer her other than conversation. And there you were, young, single, a fresh face and lean body..."

I viewed Orson in the full bloom of his unconstrained self-indulgence and resisted the urge to interrupt him.

He seemed to be listening to the echo of his own words and appeared to find them wanting. He sighed and glanced at the driver side window, realigning his thoughts.

"Jenny started out in Building 612, as you may know, before moving over to 610. I remember her first day nine years ago, that lovely smile of hers. She was a nervous little thing, thin as a rail, much thinner in those days. She wanted desperately to make a good impression. That first day she smiled at me and stuck out her hand and said, 'Hi, I'm Jenny Tristan!' I pretended I had not heard her. But why? I cannot explain it. I buried myself in the set of cabling diagrams piled on my desk. It was a shameful moment, one of my many. I thought she would never again look at me, much less smile or speak, but she did, of course, because she was Jenny.

"A few days after the funeral Marjorie and I were alone in the office. We sat across from each other discussing the beauty of a restless moonlit ocean, the treachery of rip tides, and the fragile nature of life. When we spoke of the tragedy, she said, 'Things happen for a reason, don't you see?'

"Oh, but I did not see. How many times have we heard such idle nonsense? But on her lips those words bore an inexpressible depth and conviction I had never experienced in anyone, young or old. 'What could be a valid reason for what happened to Jenny?' I asked. She said we are not meant to know everything just yet, but that you had done everything in your power to save her. She spoke as if she herself had witnessed all that happened that night."

"But you don't believe that I did all I could, do you?"

Orson hesitated. "You ask this question because of what I said before in a moment of bitterness and weakness. But you are wrong, just as you were wrong to..."

"Wrong to what?"

Orson noticed him first, the old man climbing the front steps of an apartment building across the street. The light over the door was like a rope slowly pulling him up. There seemed no end to his journey nor to the surrounding darkness.

"Certain individuals fancy themselves experts when it comes to another's trials and sorrows," Orson said. "They pass judgment. If I were in so and so's place, I would have done such and such... Hogwash! They know nothing. Such specimens are worms with wormy brains who possess one skill alone, that of pushing their tiny heads through dirt. There is more value to that old man's every step than to the accumulated accomplishments of such invertebrates."

"I was wrong to what, Orson?"

"You are a tenacious man. How to put this... It was clear to all of us how Jenny adored you. It was astonishing, actually. Believe me, I understand I am the wrong person to say this to you. In fact, it may be hypocritical of me, but it appears fate has made me the only one

145

in a position to say it, so I will. You were wrong to have taken Jenny for granted, David."

It was true. A truth shoved to the back of my consciousness, avoided, forgotten, like an old dull knife pushed to the back of a drawer. Orson had addressed me as *David* for the first time. He had drawn the knife that had lain hidden and made it sharp again, and it cut deeply into me.

But I came back to her, I wanted to explain. I made her smile. I made her laugh. I made her happy again.

I kept silent. I was ashamed.

Orson waited, feeling pity for a man he observed with a mix of envy and antipathy. I suspected he was wondering, from within the context of his own stupendous failure, if I was capable of understanding Jenny's love for me, the depth and breadth of it, a love others could only dream of. He was offering me the podium of catharsis, and if I chose not to use it, he would continue to avail himself of the unique opportunity his wife had, perhaps unwittingly, presented us both.

"Look at me," Orson said, "the suffering I have caused... One evening last month I felt an awakening of my libido in Marjorie's presence, the first time in nearly two years. I was astonished by the development, but I was discreet, of course. As fate would have it, Paulina was in Florida visiting her parents. I asked Marjorie if she would have dinner with me that Saturday. She was reluctant at first, but finally agreed, and I took her to a wonderful Italian restaurant.

"After dinner we came here to her apartment. Perhaps she too had been thinking of my situation from the moment I revealed my issue to her. Was her decision to *help me* a sacrificial offering? Despite what you might think, I harbor no illusions about myself. Marjorie helped me feel like a man again. I am convinced the only pleasure she experienced was witnessing my expression of relief as I realized my condition was temporary. It was a one-time gift, I knew. The dear girl did not have to say it."

"You're in love with her," I said.

"In a manner, I suppose. But no, it is a different love from that which I feel for Paulina. Marjorie and I are friends, nothing more. We confided in each other. You see, there is too much of Paulina in me. I am permeated with Paulina. I love her the way I love myself, and I despise her the way I despise myself. We are one and the same. Marjorie was an angel sent to me from Heaven, a friend I never deserved and whom I shall never again see. Even a pretentious boor such as myself can learn to do what is right given enough time to ponder.

"I give you my word, Pintor. I will talk to Morp and have my hours changed so that her path and mine no longer cross, or I will seek other employment. I will never see Marjorie Carlsen again in this life, I promise you."

"And Paulina?"

"Paulina knows everything. I told her I was going to end this today... No, she did not use you, not in the way you are thinking. Her uncertainty and anxiety when she spoke to you were genuine. Her suspicions, her tears, her begging, all of that was real. And thoroughly distressing to me, I might add. It was my miserable misfortune to hear it all. You see, I had returned home early from my doctor's appointment on Tuesday. I heard Paulina on the phone pleading with you. She sounded like a lovelorn schoolgirl. 'Please David, oh please.' I immediately thought of Jenny and Marjorie and now my own wife, the mystery of their attraction to you. I was confused, outraged. She was weeping as she repeated your name. I remembered the days after the funeral with anguish, not only for Jenny, but for how tenderly Paulina had spoken of you, how moved by your grief.

"She was unaware that I was standing in the hallway listening. Gradually I realized it was not all that I thought and feared, but I could not stay. I snuck out of the apartment undetected as she was ending the call. I took a walk around the block to clear my head and to allow her time to freshen up. And though I understood why she had called you, I could not forget the intimate tone of her voice as she repeated your name.

"When I went back to the apartment, I was furious, having conjured strange thoughts. I asked her why she had called you, of all people. She seemed surprised that I knew but quickly recovered. 'Why are you lying to me?' she cried out. It was then I told her about Marjorie. I had never once mentioned her name previous to that moment.

"In any case, my confession proved to be the prelude to a night of horrors. We battled from room to room, breaking objects, ripping open old wounds and gouging out new ones. It was an excruciating affair, utterly exhausting, but Paulina would not relent, demanding that I tell her everything about Marjorie, the size of her breasts and buttocks, her favorite foods, the cut and color of her hair, whether she had a nickname for me, or I for her, had she cooked for me, was she as good a cook and so on.

"Even as we lay side by side in bed, she continued her onslaught until, mercifully, she collapsed into sleep. I drifted from nightmare to nightmare, and when I woke, I found her curled against me like a child, her face swollen from weeping. I began to kiss her. She opened her eyes and we made love for the first time in nearly two years. We spoke no more of Marjorie...

"Do not think unkindly of Paulina. I left her no choice. I was thinking only of myself. Perhaps she believed you were the only person who would listen to her. Perhaps she simply needed someone to make her feel she was not alone. You will have to forgive her for not calling you back once she knew about Marjorie. I can tell you she is embarrassed by it all, by her conversation with you, her request of you, my infidelity. I believe she was hoping you would find no opportunity to discover the truth, or if you did, that you would let it be, that she would never again have to speak to you."

Orson shut off the CD player and closed his eyes. We sat awhile in silence.

I thought our encounter had come to an end. I was reaching for the passenger side door when he turned to me.

"I have something more to confess to you, Pintor. When I informed Belinda I was leaving for a meeting on Post, I could almost see your alerted and troubled expression through the cubicle wall, your reluctant spirit ceding to the call of duty. I wondered for an instant if Paulina had called you to bring you up to speed.

"Before I left the Command parking lot, I knew for sure she had not. I checked your regular parking space as I walked across the lot and saw that your car was not there. A few glances in my rearview mirror as I made my way out of the lot confirmed my suspicion that you were indeed following me.

"My hope was that you would grow tired and go away. I looked out Marjorie's window at 6:10 and saw that you had not left. I can assure you I had no desire to see you here on South Street. I thought all the while driving here, soon I will be free of this man, Paulina will never talk to him again, and Marjorie will be no more than a bittersweet memory.

"When I saw you get out of your car, I don't know what came over me. I panicked. I wanted to crawl under the floor mat. Seeing you illumined by the headlights affected me in a way I could never have imagined. I was struck by the symbolism of the moment. Something of David and Goliath stirred in my thoughts, causing me great consternation.

"I felt profound shame, and then resentment. It was as though you had claimed the moral high ground and were looking down on me, slingshot in hand. In that moment I saw you as Paulina's champion, come to restore her honor.

"It is a strange thing to ponder, I know. Utterly absurd. There is no denying I have been a terrible husband, and a weak man. I deserve neither Paulina nor Marjorie. You did not want this encounter any more than I did. And yet, there may come a day when both you and I will recognize its value."

I felt lightheaded as I stared at the shiny dashboard, my ears and cheeks warm as poached eggs. I needed a drink in the worst way and something to eat.

"Go now! Forget you ever knew Orson and Paulina Massey."

The Hollywood ring of Orson's words caused me to study his face. Had he been playing with my head all this while? No, Orson was being Orson, adding his peculiar signature to the evening.

"What happens to Marjorie?" I said.

"What happens to any of us? Paulina and I are turning a new page, writing a new story, as it were. Goodbye and good luck, Pintor. I won't see you again. I'm taking Paulina away for a couple of weeks on a long road trip. I'm sure I will not miss you."

I moved my car and Orson drove away. I thought of Marjorie sitting alone at her kitchen table trying to understand her place in the world. It was almost enough to get me to walk back to 139 South Street. I saw myself ringing her doorbell, waiting for the second-floor window to open, the warm key to fall in my hands. Would she think my visit the answer to prayer?

But it would be wrong on so many levels. I had nothing to give her. Marjorie Carlsen was a survivor, arguably an angel. She would make her way through the dark pathways of life without my assistance.

I wondered if Orson would look for another job so he wouldn't have to move two hundred miles south because of the BRAC decision. I wondered if the Massey marriage would survive over the long term.

Despite Orson's flaws, I envisioned him trudging across a vast desert in his voluminous suit, stained tie and bulging wingtips bearing the burden of love, the complicated weight of imperfect lovers and incessant bloodletting pushing his feet deeper into the sand with each step. The times I had turned Orson into a grotesque caricature in my head, or chuckled at the targeted jokes told by the usual invertebrates, now almost had the feel of sacrilege.

I had to eat something but decided to skip the food court pizza. I didn't want the cold cuts in my refrigerator to go bad, nor the lettuce. The bread was still okay but wouldn't be in another couple of days.

On my way back to the apartment I noted the shoppers and brightly lit stores. I passed *The Fox Hole's* hidden bloom of topless women and miasma of lonely men and watched the low brown building fade in my rearview mirror like a mirage.

It began to snow lightly and the windshield wipers were sweeping away the melting snowflakes. That's when I thought to write the letter.

Jenny had cried watching the movie about the girl and her dead boyfriend, the girl in her bedroom writing the letter to her dead boyfriend. "Everybody needs closure," Jenny had said wiping away tears as we walked out of the theater hand in hand.

I got to the apartment and ate a ham and salami sandwich with some lettuce and then I wrote the letter. I held nothing back, told Jenny everything I should have but never did. I went outside and walked for a while. The snowflakes were bigger and farther apart now and melted on my face and hands.

I found a quiet place. I set fire to my words and watched them float and twist and squirm.

When the last of the smoke had drifted away, I was left to wonder if there really was a warm, blue-skied Santa Cruz de Tenerife waiting for someone like me.

Swimming Lessons

OLIVIA STOPPED SMOKING last year. She also took swimming lessons at the YMWCA and does laps four days a week after work. This is what she has told him, and he has no reason to doubt her. She has lost a few pounds. Her voice is clearer too, though a little cooler than it was yesterday.

Has it been over a year?

She's become more philosophical, which is okay, but this little dinnertime funk is not what he was expecting. He'd come back to her finally and got her to smile on his third day of wooing and got her to say, "Okay, we'll go to dinner."

Despite his having dumped her.

Is that what he did? She never used that word. The breakup had been mutually agreed upon, hadn't it? She had nodded, understood, made no effort to contest his reasoning. In fact, she seemed to have been anticipating the moment. She never made a fuss about it and had maintained her dignity throughout.

As great as Olivia was, the decision had been a no-brainer. He was young and for a time enjoyed the liberties life without Olivia afforded. But what she had left inside him had spread like a fire, extinguishing the loveless thrills and pleasures of his new life.

But that is in the past. A rough stretch, to be sure, for her too, but they survived and here they are.

He teases her, trying to get her to smile. He reminds her of the times she vowed to give up margaritas and chocolate. The teasing is not making things better. He tells her, all kidding aside, it's fabulous that she's been able to conquer cigarettes. And without a patch or gum or hypnosis. Cold turkey, an act of rock-solid will. He bets she can swim like a fish too.

She gives him a look he's not used to. She never used to give him *that* look. He has to stop being the patronizing up-and-coming young project manager to her going-nowhere divorced mom secretary. He really has got to stop doing that.

"I've been painting," he offers. "Not walls. You know, like Picasso, canvas on an easel, with oils and brushes and all that jazz."

"Painting what?" she says.

He wants to say, *I've been painting you, Olivia.* Instead, he says, "Ah, different things."

"Things? Like what?"

"Uh, you know, things I want to understand better." He laughs it off and changes the subject.

They are both glad when the entrées are served. Olivia isn't really eating. She's sampling and drinking, getting lost in thought. After a while she tells him about an old woman she saw smoking outside a supermarket leaning against the wall, smoking a cigarette and watching the rain fall.

Olivia is finishing off her second martini as Nick ponders what she has just told him. He thinks this is about Olivia seeing herself in the future, but doesn't want to say that to her. He feels a sharp pain in his chest imagining her like that, alone, her lungs being eaten away.

He lubricates the mouth of his third beer bottle with a wedge of lime and is thinking how he wants to get back to saying more about his painting.

He wants to explain how it really has everything to do with her, Olivia, when a big-legged country girl wearing a tiny denim skirt appears on the scene, trailed by a hulking cowboy.

The first thing the young lady does upon settling into her seat is locate the closest viable male. She locks eyes with Nick just a little too long. Nick feels exposed as he turns back to Olivia who is asking him a question.

"How old would you say Nicole's receptionist is?"

"Who?"

"You know who I'm talking about."

"You mean the new girl at BMD? Uh, no idea, what, twenty-six?"

"Thirty-one," she says with a hard smile that fades as she looks away.

That would be Evelyn Ortiz in the cafeteria blushing like a schoolgirl waving hi to Nick as if Olivia did not exist—and just minutes after Olivia had smiled and said, "Okay, we'll go to dinner."

Nick squeezes the bridge of his nose.

"How is Cody?" he says.

Olivia shakes her head, disgusted with herself for bringing up the pretty receptionist.

"He'll be moving into his dorm room end of August."

"Whoa, a son in college! I guess I knew, but wow. You must be so proud."

She looks up, dejected.

"Big things in store for the young man," Nick says.

"He's not in a good place."

"What do you mean?"

"He's just so angry all the time."

"Oh, that, yeah. Teenage boys. When things don't line up just right for them. I remember so many triggers at that age. You never know what'll set a kid off. I wouldn't worry too much about it, Olivia, it's just a phase."

She peers inside him for a moment, goes back to studying her flan and begins to slice it in thin curved slivers with her spoon. She curve-slices, watches the moist amber slivers flop to the plate, then crosshatches them into tiny pieces.

"What kinds of things?" Olivia says looking up.

A slow voluptuous shifting begins in the corner of his left eye.

"Things?"

"What things are you painting?"

The girl crosses her big legs in slow motion, diverting Nick for an instant. Olivia turns her head, catches a glimpse of the ascending flesh, the disappearing skirt, and the amused triumphant eyes.

Olivia looks at Nick with a broken smile.

AFTER THE BREAKUP, Nick had begun to frequent bars on weekends. One evening, nearly a year in, he met Meryl, who was drinking a glass of red wine at the bar. She was cool, independent and devoted to *compassionate detachment*, as she put it. She described herself as a Buddhist Christian or Christian Buddhist. He couldn't remember. Nick and Meryl had their fun, and one day he texted her, *Goodbye M*, and she texted back, *but hav sir prize 4 u N! c u fri?*

Against his better judgment, Nick drove to Meryl's apartment that Friday after work. Jade, whom he'd never met, was the *sir prize*. She led him by the hand into Meryl's bedroom.

"Where's Meryl?" Nick said.

"She told me you have a hole in your life."

"Meryl told you that?"

"It's not like she had to."

"So we've known each other how long?"

"It's not about time, Nick."

"Doesn't everyone have a hole in his life?"

"*Her* life."

"Doesn't everyone have a hole in *her* life?"

"Oh sure, it's just that some holes are bigger than others."

Later, he caught Meryl in the doorway video-recording the occasion with her smart phone. He shouted at both women with alarming vigor, frightening them. He calmed down, got dressed, apologized and left.

Nick drove into town, left his car parked and started to walk. He wandered about without any thought as to where he was going. It was nice out and quiet on the streets. When he came upon *Moonlight Art Supplies* it seemed to him he had been walking toward that place all his life.

He stopped before the display window and stared at a half-finished portrait of an ordinary-looking woman with a wounded expression that reminded him of Olivia. At the foot of the easel was a beginner's oil painting kit. Feeling suddenly driven with purpose, he walked inside the shop, purchased the kit, an easel, and an armful of rolled-up canvases, and walked out as the proprietor flipped the *Closed* sign on the glass and wood door.

Nick wanted to make sense of the turmoil Olivia was causing inside him. He dedicated many hours to painting her from memory. At first he painted only the shadowed contours of her face. He painted in the color of memory, burnt sienna.

It proved to be hard, dispiriting work. He was unsure of himself, stilted. His hand, like his mind, felt like a claw at times, and at other times like water. But he persisted, moving paint from tube to palette to canvas, mixing, sweeping, dabbing, tapering, pecking, progressing from Olivia's head to other parts of her body, all rendered in the dim brown light of sleep, the smooth curve of a hip, her slightly asymmetrical mouth, a curled hand.

One night he stood on a chair and pinned all his canvases to his bedroom ceiling. He lay on his back staring at the inchoate shapes spawned by his self-deception. He tossed and turned all night. In the morning, he took the canvasses down, crushed them like fallen leaves and deposited them inside two large plastic bags for disposal.

The next night he dreamed he was drowning, and no one but Olivia took notice. He woke up in a sweat and found photographs of Olivia in his night table and made those his new starting point, adding the colors of day to his renderings.

But neither inspiration nor ability graced his efforts, and he ended each night staring at his hands as though the multicolored stains were the spilled blood of his lost days. This was the price for moving forward, he decided.

Whether motivated by willfulness, love, or despair, the difficulty of painting Olivia Tully was the force that finally drove him back to her.

OLIVIA EXCUSES HERSELF. There is a curious vibrating quality to Nick's gaze as he monitors Olivia's unsteady walk to the Ladies Room.

He's lost her. She has realized it is all a mistake. He is a hopeless case, a cripple stumbling between two worlds, and one of them has nothing to do with her. She's always known it, hasn't she? So why did she agree to any of this?

He downs a shot of bourbon and, pushed by a sudden wave of self-loathing, ventures more deeply into forbidden terrain. Those meaty legs, those big entangled fleshy creatures, are undoubtedly poised to spring forth from beneath that table to devour him.

So it is that the observer is being observed, he notes upon looking up. Of course, of course.

And the temptress is reduced to giggles.

The cowboy boyfriend doesn't get the joke, being always a step behind. Not so much a puppy dog as a lust lackey, but one gloriously primed to break the random jaw at the faintest insinuation or imagined trespass.

Why is she giggling? Does he make her nervous? Not likely. She is seeing it all played out, isn't she? The boyfriend leaping up to defend her right to giggle, his fist breaking Nick's jaw, Nick actually being okay with that...

Is it his fault Olivia met someone else first, had a son with someone who never loved her, or that she embarked on a journey earmarked for disaster? Who appointed him her savior anyway?

He watches Olivia walk back from the Ladies Room. Her shoulders are hunched with tension. She looks exhausted. The lines around her eyes have deepened, and her uneven mouth sags a bit.

"Good of you to come back," he says without smiling. "You look like you've just been to your best friend's funeral."

She's not going to sit. She stares at him in disbelief, shakes her head. "We should get going. I have to get back to Cody."

"But you told him not to wait up, didn't you?"

She doesn't answer.

"Olivia?"

"What?"

"Let's go to the multiplex. Let's go see *La La Land*. Why not?"

"This isn't funny."

"No, not trying to be, just trying to—"

"This was a bad idea."

Okay, maybe, so why is she just standing there? She looks away, narrows her eyes as if she's reading something on the far wall. Her trembling fingertips slide back and forth over the table's edge. Nick stands up, takes her ice-cold hands. Her knees buckle. He feels like he's been stabbed in the heart as he puts his arms around her.

People turn to look. The girl says something to the boyfriend, who turns his head looking outraged but baffled.

Nick leaves money under a beer bottle and takes Olivia away. Out in the parking lot they lean back against his car and Olivia lights up a cigarette. She jokes about this being the absolute last smoke she will ever have.

Nick chuckles joylessly. The sterile parking lot lights mar her features with unflattering shadows. It is just too much. The suicidal cigarette, the cruel lighting, the prickling humidity.

It is all too much and he doesn't know what this means for them. He looks away, imagining Evelyn Ortiz walking toward him under these same lights, her small, firm breasts bobbing like mangos, her *Café au lait*-colored skin clear and smooth, her entire bearing somehow magically enriched by the same otherwise damning lights.

"I can't see the stars," Nick says. "These stupid lights. These ugly buildings. These toxin-spewing cars. All this crap always getting in the way of seeing what's beautiful. For the love of mercy, Olivia, I can't see the freaking stars!"

"The air conditioning," she counters softly. "I was freezing in that place."

"I'm so glad we're out of there. Did you like the food?"

"The food was okay."

"What about the company?"

"Damn you, Nick. You break my heart."

"What? Oh, come on."

"You're such a jerk."

"I know... But Olivia, listen, why don't we forget the movie? Let's go to the beach. Let's go where we can see the stars."

"And the moon. And the waves too."

"What about Cody?"

"It's all right. I told him not to wait up. Don't you remember? I'll make him chocolate chip pancakes in the morning."

"Come here, darling."

She tosses the cigarette to the ground and before she can crush it he takes her in his arms and kisses her on the mouth. He can't remember the last time he's kissed a woman like that.

Wrong. He can. About a year ago.

She presses herself against him, and they kiss. A long kiss stopped by a honking car passing by. They look at one another, smile. She snuggles like a kitten against him, and he can't stop kissing her strangely pretty, smiling face.

OLIVIA INFORMS HIM she has never once stood on a beach at night. He glances at her, amazed. She sparkles with excitement. Evelyn the receptionist, the big-legged flirt, the clueless boyfriend, the breakup, all of it gone, at least for tonight. He draws Olivia close and kisses her as if she were his only source of sustenance.

"You taste so good," he says.

They remove their shoes and walk barefoot on the cool white sand hand in hand, leaning into the thick, briny wind and watching the black and silver breakers surge and crash.

Olivia lets go his hand and releases her hair and it whips about like a blazing new life form.

"I've never seen so many stars," she says and points her finger. "Look at the moon, Nick."

"The moon and us, Livy."

She chuckles. "So, I'm Livy now?" She snatches his hand, kisses it and runs toward the water.

"Will you say it, then?" she shouts turning her head, running.

"Hey, wait, will I say what?"

She starts singing *Love Me Do*, or something else, or it could be the wind or the surf, or maybe he heard the song earlier and it's playing in his head.

He begins to sing it too, and in a little while he will say *it*, finally.

He loves looking at her, the way the star-drunk night cradles her, the way he would have painted her. In a little while he will say it, finally, and she will know it for sure and he will know it too.

Olivia drops her skirt and they become quiet. She unbuttons her blouse, undoes her bra and tosses blouse and bra to the wind. Nick cranks out more *Love Me Do*, refining his delivery with each verse, feeling the confident joy of the song and what it is leading up to. She slips off her panties and flips them in his direction and extends her arms like a show host introducing an incomparable celebrity to an exuberant audience, *Ladies and gentlemen, I bring you*—

In the moonlight her body glows like polished alabaster.

"This moment!" he cries. "If I could paint you, if I just had the talent to paint you just as you are this moment..." She glances at him wondering what he is saying. He points at her as if he were on a stage, in a musical. "Though I got no paint no brush no talent even, I got you, Livy!"

Something flies into his eye. He rubs his eyeball and feels a sudden chill.

"I love you, Nick!" Olivia shouts and dashes toward the surf.

"Hey, just you wait a second, young lady!"

She stops at the edge of the water, looks down, and with the side of her foot carves a groove in the wet scurrying sand. Nick demands of his fingers serenity, unbuttons and tosses his shirt and drops his pants as Olivia steps into the waters.

A wave sweeps over her thighs and drags her in nearly to her waist. She screams in delight and staggers back toward the shore, twisting to see Nick stumbling toward her, pants wrapped around his ankles like a lasso. It makes her laugh when he falls and sand sticks to the side of his face. Nick watches Olivia laugh from an abundance of happiness, and it makes him laugh too.

She turns and talks to the ocean, and Nick swears the waters have listened and, in obedience, have grown placid. A strange and lovely stillness settles around Olivia. He could stay like this forever, looking up at her from the cool damp sand.

Her arms drawn back like angel wings, she wades into the waters to mid-thigh, a pale Renoir nude bending at the waist, petting the smooth wide heaving surface.

And then she is gone!

Sucked gone eaten gone swallowed gone.

Deafening adrenaline storm, pants and boxers yanked and tossed, sand-spitting dash and breathless leap.

The riptide yields a thousand shadows, his father's face and garbled words:

stay calm locate stay calm swim parallel locate shore are you listening Nicolás?

up, up, up, breathe, breathe, breathe

where is she, she, she

stay calm

Livy please, please

stay calm locate swim Livy parallel please

going down

no please

down please no down no

Nick... Nick... Nick...

. . . . .

"What's he saying?"

"Don't know, grab her, will you?"

"Sandy, no! Bad girl! No, Sandy!"

"He's going to be okay, Miss."

On her knees stooped over, cheek against his cheek, her hand on his chest.

"You dummy, didn't I tell you I took swimming lessons?"

"Sandy, come on, stop being such a pain—!"

"Put the collar on her."

"You scared the hell out of me, Nick."

"Let's go gather up their clothes."

"Big wet tongue."

"Nicky? What did you say?"

"Sandy a good girl. She love me."

"Yeah, Nick."

"But I love *you*, Livy."

"Did you just...? You do?"

"Yeah, yes, uh-huh."

"Nicky."

"I would have died for you, Livy."
"Oh, Nick, but you did. You died for me."

The Real World

AMADOR WOKE UP to a blizzard the Monday of his job interview at the button factory. He was to be there 9:00 AM sharp, but looking out the window of his basement apartment, he deemed it unlikely.

A winter wonderland, he thought, and felt a happy tickling in his belly and a vague sense of unmerited but welcomed gain that was about to translate into precious hours of reading, writing, and puttering. A good tickly warm feeling like in the old days sitting at the kitchen table with Ma listening to the litany of closures being announced by the local radio station.

"Jefferson Street Elementary, closed. Sycamore Vocational, closed. *Lafayette Street Elementary,* closed!"

Yes! Yes! Yes! Oh, hallelujah, yes!

The snow swept across his line of sight in horizontal sheets. Eight inches, at least, with no end in sight.

A snowbound car parked just out front peeked out at him through a shrinking passenger side window. For an instant, he thought he saw a pair of eyes trained on him. It made no sense, he knew, but the mere suggestion of being watched tempered his enthusiasm.

He went into the hallway and opened the front door to get a better look. The swirling snow had gathered in a coiffed sweep in the cellar's stairwell tunnel, rising up against the foundation wall. He poked his head out of the stairwell and saw no one, but he was beset with doubt.

Not taking any chances, he called the factory and was stunned to hear a woman's voice. When he explained who he was, and that he wanted to reschedule his interview because of the snowstorm, the lady, whose face he imagined being big and round, laughed with gusto.

"Did you say it was snowing, darling?"

She let Amador chew on that for a moment. "I'm just busting you, hon. In Minneapolis we call this, flurries."

"But this is Newark," Amador said.

"Is it? Oh, my..."

Lee Anne cautioned that he should give himself plenty of time given that management maintained and enforced a strict zero tolerance policy for tardiness *and* for indecent behavior.

He put on the hooded coat Maggie got him for Christmas and a pair of his father's old dust-covered galoshes that he dug up in the subterranean workshop adjacent to his living quarters and made his way through the blinding snow. What should have been a thirty-minute walk turned into an hour-long odyssey, and his pants were soaked to mid-thigh by the time he walked into the reception area of the factory minutes before his appointment.

Lee Anne looked far more refined than Amador had imagined. She gave him a big welcoming smile and made a phone call. A man named Grover appeared a minute later and escorted him to a deserted corner of a large open studio and told him to have a seat at a long white table. From there Amador was able to observe a number of men and women bent over drafting tables like scribes. Two men and a woman were huddled together in one corner. One of the men broke in his direction. The man was in his mid to late forties, balding and with glasses. He approached with his back and arms slightly arched, and his head down, as if he was looking for something he had lost. He must have been a wrestler once, probably in high school, maybe in college.

The man sat across from Amador at the long white table and studied a sheet that Amador recognized as his resume. The man looked up and said, "Amador Santiago?" in a way that seemed to upset him, though he had pronounced his name almost as well as any Spaniard. Amador nodded and said yes, and the man flipped over the resume and pushed it toward him across the table blank side up. He took a freshly sharpened pencil from his shirt pocket, placed it on the table and pushed the pencil toward Amador.

"Draw a circle," he said. "Three-inch diameter."

Amador hesitated, as though expecting a ruler or compass to be provided. "Freehand," the man said.

So Amador drew the circle, which came out better than he could have hoped. The man stared with intensity at Amador's circle.

"Draw a circle around it, five and one-half-inch diameter, same center point," the man said without looking up from the sheet. He watched Amador's hand go round and complete the new circle. The man then extended his own hand across the table, causing Amador to reciprocate thinking he was being congratulated on getting the job, but the man just wanted his pencil back.

The man took the pencil from Amador's hand, put it back in his shirt pocket, folded Amador's resume, got up and started walking away. Amador wondered what about those concentric circles, or him, had prompted his interviewer to leave so abruptly and without a word. But before Amador could formulate a theory, the man stopped, looked back over his shoulder and said, "You'll start tomorrow, 7:00 AM sharp."

In that moment all things seemed possible to Amador, but he maintained his composure. No smile, no thank you. A mere nod of the head to let the man know he understood. Then he sat at the long white table, feeling strangely empowered, but just as strangely at a loss as to what to do next. He waited for Grover to come by with papers and to impart a word or two of guidance, but Grover never appeared, nor did anyone else. After a while Amador got up and found his way back out into the blizzard.

RAMIRO AND PILAR wanted their son to have every advantage they never had, so they had Amador live rent-free in the basement of their two-family row house. Ramiro had sectioned off a portion of the basement and prepared the tiny apartment while Amador was away at school completing his Bachelor's degree.

In the winter of 1976 Amador no longer owned a car, nor did he have regular access to one. Given his circumstances and all that had happened, he felt that a half-hour walk to work (under normal weather conditions) was a small price to pay for his previous miscalculations.

His first morning at Smart Buttons Lee Anne smiled and told him not to take any chances and to make sure he always clocked in *before* 7:00 AM unless he wanted to have a half-day's pay docked.

Amador found his way to the design studio without Grover or anyone else's assistance. He idled about awhile, but no one spoke to him. Finally, a plodding, heavy-limbed woman approached him. With a stern and skeptical air she said, "I'm well aware the word *amador* is Spanish for *lover*." She said this as though he were a lothario on the prowl and that she was on to him, so he better watch his step.

The woman guffawed before Amador could respond. "I'm just busting you. Elaine Sudwicks. I'm your manager."

She was the second person in as many days to "bust" him, so he prepared mentally for that type of exchange whenever he met someone for the first time at the button factory. It was Elaine who informed him that the man who had interviewed him was the owner of *Sharp Buttons, Inc.*, Mr. Nadelman.

While Elaine was showing Amador around, Mr. Nadelman walked by. His eyes scoured the floor just as when Amador had first laid eyes on him. Elaine drew her head close to Amador's and somberly confided, "You see him over there? You wouldn't know it by his demeanor, but just between you and I, that man there is a hopeless bleeding-heart *weenie.*"

A weenie, was he?

Amador struck down the impulse to laugh. He was not sure how to interpret Elaine's remark. Was she being serious? He smiled uncertainly as he studied her face and realized she was not kidding. A glint of satisfaction in her eye suggested some form of kinship had been established between them, some shared understanding regarding all that was wrong with the world. Additionally, an invitation of a sort seemed implied.

Should he say something to her, set her straight? Gently explain they were not of like mind...? But on his first day of work?

Then something in her changed, or maybe he had been misreading her all along, because suddenly he glimpsed a ray of bitterness in her eye.

Was he imagining it? No, no, it was there, all right, the mocking eye, the one that said, *You didn't earn this job. What you did was satisfy a weenie-brained quota requirement in Nadelman's stupid ass bleeding-heart mind.*

AMADOR WORKED in the graphics department of the button factory. He would be spending most of his time in the darkroom adjacent to the design studio developing negatives and prints of the artwork that was created to go on the buttons.

These were not dress buttons but the kind that have nifty slogans on them like *Virginia Is for Lovers* or *I'd Rather Be Hunting*. The more popular buttons had a genial, cartoonish quality to them, like the one of Bambi's head and its long red tongue hanging out the back of a pickup truck. Those kinds of buttons.

Amador always looked for reasons to like people. Despite his earlier reservations about Elaine, he called Maggie to tell her Elaine had actually said something nice to him. She had informed him that Mr. Nadelman told her that Amador had a very good eye and that, in time, he could become a real asset to Sharp Buttons.

Furthermore, Mr. Nadelman wanted Leo Mancini to teach Amador whatever he needed to know to manage the darkroom and to get him up to speed on basic layout and design work.

With his goatee, wavy long black hair, and extravagance of expression, Leo reminded Amador of a musketeer. He was in his early forties and had recently come into a quarter of a million-dollar inheritance with the passing of his diabetic mother.

"Welcome to the Twilight Zone, my man," Leo said the first time he took Amador into the darkroom.

In the psychoactive red light, he showed Amador how to develop negatives and transfer the images to paper. He said you had to refine your sensitivities to get it right, and you had to woo time.

Leo grasped a negative with a pair of plastic tongs and gently agitated it in the developer tray for a few seconds and showed Amador what he should look for, that point where the image was just starting to darken in the darkest shadow parts but had not gotten totally black in the lightest highlight areas. The aim was to capture the detail as truly as possible in both the light and the dark.

Like so many things in life, getting it just right was a balancing act and timing was paramount. You wanted to stop everything right then and there when it was right, he said, like when you've reached that moment of moments when you're making love with the right woman. That moment was as real as it got, and you didn't want it to end. You wanted to preserve it, package it, immortalize it, but there's no stop bath tray in the bedroom, and no fixer solution to make it stick.

Leo explained to Amador that everything in life was either a moving toward that moment or a moving away from it. He wasn't talking just about sex, but about human relationship and everyday living and art and music and God.

"What the hell is the point of living if you're not always moving toward perfection?" Leo would say.

He told Amador he was leaving Sharp Buttons end of April. First thing he was going to do was fly down to Jeréz de la Frontera in Southern Spain to experience some real flamenco. He wanted to head over to Algeciras too, where he hoped to catch a brilliant young guitarist named Paco de Lucía, who was doing exciting new things and stretching the boundaries of flamenco guitar. Then he was going to hit a few jazz clubs in Paris and get back to Pamplona in time to run with the bulls.

He said he had always thought a lot about the link between flamenco and jazz and that he wanted to explore that connection. He wanted to write a book about that one day.

"Look, man, I could give a shit about money," he once told Amador. "Don't get me wrong, insofar as it buys me time, yeah, I'll take some, but sell your soul for cash? You kidding me?"

Leo's last words to Amador as he gave him a parting bearhug were, "Watch your back, my man." He glanced in Elaine's direction and stuck a folded envelope in Amador's shirt pocket.

After Leo left, Amador opened the envelope. Inside was a one-thousand dollar check payable to *Amador Santiago* and a hand-written admonition:

There's never a good reason to eat shit.

His first day alone in the darkroom Amador was determined to honor Leo by listening to the progressive jazz station his mentor had prescribed, but the static-heavy music coming out of the beat-up clock radio with its seemingly random flights of gloom, hysteria, ecstasy and slumber made him anxious.

He listened carefully for perfection, but each time he thought he was getting close, he would find himself slipping and falling, as if he were treading an icy uphill path. The effort left him jittery and troubled. Leo's favorite station gave him no peace. He tuned in to a rock and roll station that came in nice and clear. Rock was good too, and the best of it, like the best of anything else, could put you right where you needed to be.

For the most part, Amador was content with how things were going. Nobody bothered him, and the scriptorium-like isolation of the darkroom accommodated his introverted nature nicely.

After a number of weeks performing his routines and daily tasks without a hitch or a hindrance, Amador began to regard Leo's parting exhortation, *Watch your back, my man!* as borderline ludicrous. He loved Leo, but maybe his friend had spent too many hours in the darkroom.

When Amador saw the cartoonish images for the new *Don't Lose Your Head!* button (shiny guillotine, *oops*-faced prisoner, grinning executioner) emerging under the red light in the developer tray, he recognized Leo's face in both prisoner and executioner. The association was troubling, and he began to wonder if too much time spent in a darkroom could lead to warping of the brain.

Amador also began to view Elaine in a different light. His aloof manager seemed to exist in her own separate world much of the time. She didn't have a husband, boyfriend or any friend at all, that he was aware of, and he had developed a soft spot for her.

On one occasion he heard Rick Paxton and Troy Bagatelle joking about Elaine's habit of *presenting rearward*, as they put it, a reference to the suggestive way she sat on her stool while working at her drafting table.

Amador didn't appreciate the remark and almost called them out, but decided against it as both Rick and Troy had always treated him in a friendly manner, and besides, he didn't want to come across as a sanctimonious jerk.

Every day at three o'clock Amador would emerge from the darkroom squinting, his head stuffed with chemical fumes and the tinny echoes of rock and roll. He would walk past Rick and Troy and Elaine and all the others on his way to his desk to perform quality assurance tasks.

No one ever said anything to him during those walks. He must have seemed like a man released from a dungeon, slow-footed and mute, slightly disoriented. It was a quiet walk and he was usually thinking about quit time and maybe some poem about Maggie that he was working through.

One day as he was passing by, Elaine, without lifting her head, said in a voice loud enough for all to hear, "Oh my, look what the cat drug in."

An odd unprovoked remark, to be sure, but noting the smile on Elaine's face, Amador smiled back and shrugged his shoulders like a good sport.

That afternoon, just before quit time, Elaine asked Amador to draw a Conestoga wagon, which she said she needed right away. Though recognizable, Amador's wagon failed to possess the plump buoyancy Elaine was looking for. She didn't say anything when he handed her the drawing. She just set it aside.

Amador passed by Elaine's drafting table the next morning on his way to the darkroom and saw the wagon she had expected, but which he had been incapable of producing, tacked to a corner of her table. Amador guessed she had whipped it up herself in a matter of minutes last night just before calling it a day. The smug little wagon seemed to stare at him with Elaine's face. It seemed to whisper to him as he walked by, *Oh my, look what the cat drug in.*

Later that day, again just before quit time, Elaine called Amador over and asked him to draw a cheerleader waving pompoms over her head. She said she needed it right away. Amador went back to his desk and consulted Leo's parting note: *There's never a good reason to eat shit.*

It took Amador less than two minutes. His halfhearted effort drew longer than expected scrutiny from Elaine, whose Dutch boy haircut Amador had rendered flawlessly on the ungainly cheerleader's head.

Things went south from there. Amador had had it with Elaine's unrelenting litany of snide remarks and unfunny jokes at his expense and those last-minute assignments that set him up for failure and humiliation.

One late afternoon Elaine called an impromptu meeting of the graphic design team. They all stood in front of her drafting table. She made it known she wanted to "nip in the butt" the decline in the quality of work produced over the past several months. She shot a *sorry-just-had-to* smirk in Amador's direction as she displayed his wanting depiction of the Conestoga wagon as Exhibit A.

Everyone gazed at Amador, who looked as though he had just stepped out of the darkroom and had not yet adjusted to the ways of other humans. Then slowly his right hand opened wide and rose toward Elaine palm up in what seemed to all a gesture of entreaty. Amador stared at the fading light of Elaine's smirk in silence and all the graphic designers watched Amador's outer fingers curl in and his middle finger spring up straight and true as a flag post.

From about a dozen feet away Amador aligned the middle finger directly over Elaine's nose like the vertical crosshair of a riflescope and locked it in position for a full six seconds. From the corner of his eye Amador noted Rick Paxton and Troy Bagatelle exchanging celebratory glances. Having completed its mission, the finger bowed and the hand drifted back to Amador's side.

Elaine, looking *nipped in the butt*, locked her eyes on Amador. She took a moment to collect herself and then said, in a sensible enough voice, "I'm sorry, but that is just unacceptable. As you well know, Smart Buttons Inc. maintains and enforces a zero-tolerance policy for indecent behavior. You leave me no choice. You're fired. Please gather up your things and leave the premises immediately."

Amador spent a whole lot of time trying to figure out why Elaine hated him and finally gave up. Whatever the reason was, what he did to her in front of all those people probably bothered him more than it bothered Elaine, but he had no way of knowing for sure.

He had no problem getting fired, he told Maggie. He had understood and accepted Elaine's decision without protest. He deserved his punishment. He had lost his cool and had allowed his pride to get the better of him, so getting *laid off* came as a big surprise.

Lee Anne called him the next day, told him Mr. Nadelman had decided to lay him off rather than have him on the books as having been fired, meaning he would be able to collect unemployment benefits. Good old Mr. Nadelman. Still, Amador thought it best to keep the news from Ramiro and Pilar. What rationale could he provide? How would he explain to them that he was fired for giving his manager the finger in front of a roomful of people?

Day by day he was getting better at seeing things from his parents' perspective. How had four years of paying for room and board and tuition and books and travel produced two job losses and a totaled car in a span of four months? Such a return on investment might turn the most optimistic parent into a cynic.

Every day he ran his index finger down the rows of classified ads, read books, jotted down ideas for a novel about a brilliant recluse who has begun to suspect he is a ghost, and started thinking seriously about proposing to Maggie Sheehan.

IT WAS A TRICKY START to life in *the real world*, a collision of dreams and doubts. Had he committed an inexcusable blunder?

Amador thought about this a lot. Soon after graduating from college, a childhood friend of the Santiagos from back in Spain, the artist Antón Rúa, was having lunch with a friend in New York City. The friend was the famous architect, Bryson Nethercott.

Nethercott had become a fan of Rúa's ink and watercolor depictions of Galician fishermen and women dressed in the black of mourning. Nethercott became a patron of Rúa's work and a frequent visitor to the coastal villages of northwestern Spain where the Rúa and Santiago roots extended back centuries.

Rúa had spoken to Nethercott about Amador and told Ramiro that an apprenticeship in the architect's firm in Manhattan was Amador's for the asking. He gave Ramiro Nethercott's business card. Nethercott himself had circled his office phone number with red ink. Amador should call Nethercott Monday morning, Rúa told Ramiro.

It seemed a dream come true to the Santiagos. Neither Ramiro nor Pilar could sleep that night. They could not wait to tell their son the good news. To their surprise and dismay, Amador showed no interest whatsoever. On the contrary, he seemed troubled by what they were saying to him.

When they had finished talking, he explained that he had just accepted an offer to become a *Marketing Specialist* for a large company. He had bought a used Toyota Corona with the money he had borrowed from his parents and had made his first payment on his auto insurance. And now this? What would be the point of having a car if he worked in Manhattan?

It was a flimsy argument, the Santiagos knew, but *Marketing Specialist* did have a certain ring to it. It sounded important to them, in the vague way complex sophisticated jobs can. Amador told them it was a fifteen-minute drive to work and pointed out the difficulties of commuting daily to Manhattan.

The Santiagos listened, reluctant to raise any objection their college-educated son might deem old-fashioned and out of touch. They had sacrificed long and hard to raise and educate their American son and were deeply invested in his presumed ability to navigate the intricate terrain of white-collar America.

Their initial disappointment was only slightly alleviated as Amador articulated what they were both beginning to consider: they lived in a land of milk and honey. Their son was free to choose between two job opportunities so soon after earning his college degree. They knew firsthand how hard it was to make a living. And not just them. They thought of childhood friends, many of whom had left their homes in Spain to search for work in Northern Europe, Latin America, and the tristate area of the USA, spending long months at a time and even years away from their families.

Amador did not lie to his parents. He did, however, use their respectful reticence to his advantage. If they had forced the issue, he would have revealed to them his true reason for declining the architect's offer. First, he was not ready to wear a monkey suit at this point in his life, and second, and more importantly, he was unwilling to undergo the daily scrutiny of his every word, act and gesture by the friend of a friend of the family.

Would his father have tossed him out onto the street for saying such things? He didn't think so, but every man had his limits.

Though both Pilar and Ramiro had questions whirling in their heads, they decided then and there to probe no further. What good could come of it? Were they prepared to call into question their college-educated son's ability to court the American Dream? Did they really want to discover that Amador's work was to consist of installing cigarette racks and assembling carton displays in super-markets and convenience stores all across New Jersey and Staten Island?

When Amador called Maggie to inform her of his decision to decline the apprenticeship, he thought the phone line had gone dead. Finally, she told him the Corona did not seem suited for the daily rigors of transporting metal racks, shelving materials and sheets of Plexiglas. He assured her it was a temporary job, just until he could find something more suitable. He told her he just needed to be able to breathe and think.

After weeks of logging hundred plus mile days, the brakes on the Corona began to grind and the soft balding tires looked ready to explode one after another. To make things more interesting, the car would stall for no apparent reason at random times, particularly during downpours and ice storms. On top of that, the sudden onset one day of a pots and pans rattling noise in the car's rear end made Amador feel as though the bottom of his world was literally going to drop out.

The unexpectedly steep cost of auto repairs and maintenance, the liability insurance, the money owed to his financially strapped parents, and the not so small matter of buying Maggie's engagement ring led Amador to conclude he wasn't earning nearly enough to meet his current and future needs. He began scrutinizing the classifieds with a sharpened eye, lingering over potential job opportunities he had previously dismissed out of hand, reading between the lines, imagining himself working with purpose.

In February of 1976, driving south on the New Jersey Parkway, the Corona slid off an exit ramp onto a snowy bank and no sooner had it come to a stop than it was knocked in the rear.

It didn't feel like much of a collision to Amador, but when he got out, he noted the snaggle-toothed right fender and bent hood of the Porsche. The spoiled jewel of a car made the barely scratched Corona look regal by contrast.

A man in a suit, tie and unbuttoned overcoat emerged from the Porsche whimpering, "Oh shit! Oh shit!" but he was quickly reduced to silence. He looked like a man who had just come upon a bloodied relative lying in a gutter.

When he reached inside his coat, Amador braced himself. The man drew out his wallet and handed Amador one-hundred and fifty-three dollars. He told Amador he preferred keeping the insurance companies out of it. Amador took the money and they went their separate ways.

That was when Amador decided he had had his fill of being a Marketing Specialist. On his way home he dropped off all his tools and equipment at the tobacco company office and told his manager he would not be coming back. He was sorry for not giving two-weeks' notice, but he was dealing with a family crisis. He hoped he would understand.

What Amador said to his manager wasn't altogether untrue. The awkward fix he found himself in while living in the basement of his parents' apartment house had to be taken into account.

Amador had the brakes and rear end fixed, the small dent in the rear fender hammered out, and new tires mounted and balanced. Troubleshooting was performed to determine the cause of all the stalling episodes, a corroded ground as it turned out.

While the car was at the mechanic's shop, he decided to get a complete tune-up and an oil change, and had the car vacuumed and washed inside and out.

He got the car back late on a Thursday and called Maggie to tell her the Corona was shining like the sun and that he wanted to take her out to dinner Friday. He was holding her engagement ring as he talked to her, though he kept it a secret. It was to be a surprise, after all, as was the five-hundred dollars he had put into a 36-month CD for their future together.

Despite the $1350 he had handed the mechanic, Amador felt that everything was going to work out just fine. He felt an enormous sense of relief now that everything was coming into focus, and he could not contain his joy.

"I am happy as a monkey, Maggie Sheehan," he quipped, which made Maggie laugh.

He told her he had a job interview Monday morning for a position in the graphics department at Sharp Buttons, Inc. The job would pay him thirty-five percent more than what he had been making at the tobacco company!

When Maggie questioned his optimism, he insisted the job was his to lose and gave Maggie three reasons. First, he had minored in *Graphic Design* (to appease his parents, having thrown them for a loop with his choice of English as his major). Second, the Sharp

Buttons building was nestled in a hopelessly depressed part of town (reducing the competition). And third, no one wanted or needed the job more than he did. On his way to see Maggie in his shiny, clean-smelling Corona that Friday, Amador pictured himself on one knee prying open the velvet blue ring case.

He would later explain to his bride-to-be that because he had been so deeply immersed in the beauty and promise of the moment, he had been only *marginally* aware that the traffic lights at the intersection by the mechanic's shop were down. He told Maggie the car ahead of him had rolled on through the intersection without the slightest hesitation, and the Corona had followed as though being tugged along by the larger vehicle.

Later, while staring at the fingernail gashes in his palms from squeezing the Corona steering wheel during impact he wondered, what were the odds that as harebrained an individual as himself would come speeding down the cross-road to his left, slam into the Corona and send it flying into the rear of Antonio Ventoso's parked tow truck?

Maggie, are you there? Are you there, Maggie?

All she could bring herself to say was, "I love you, Amador."

MAGGIE HAS RECENTLY been thinking about things that fly. A flock of blackbirds, a skirmish of robins, a trio of fruit flies hovering over the kitchen sink.

She and Amador have a large post and rail fenced backyard. Their neighbor owns several acres of land behind them. The hawks are drawn to the open spaces and soar above the properties looking for prey. The hawks are beautiful to watch, though menacing.

Maggie considers how the days and the seasons fly by. She often reminisces. She sees the front of Amador's Corona lifting, turning and flying into the rear of a tow truck all those years ago, sees the dinner plate flying past Amador's head and crashing with a dull thud against the kitchen wall of her in-laws' apartment.

Maggie and Amador are selling their home of thirty years, it being time to tighten the belt given Amador has lost his job at *Real World Solutions* due to a higher purpose and for the greater good.

RWS has been downsizing, merging, buying back stock, downsizing, merging, buying back stock, etcetera at a vertiginous rate, truly something to behold. That and how keenly determined RWS is to bump up the quality of life of all the good folks grinding it out in *The Real World*.

Increased revenues, lowered debt, record profits, etcetera, all thanks to the hard work, gumption, loyalty, etcetera of the beautiful AKPs (i.e., Ass-Kicking People) who make *Real World Solutions* what RWS is all about, as per email with ode-like subject line, "In Praise of AKPs," from the company president, I.M. Goody, which Amador took his time reading on his laptop screen before going home his last day of work at RWS, where the future has never been brighter.

Real World Solutions for people living in The Real World!

Amador sees the past in Maggie's face. She sees it in his face. Sometimes the past flows into the present like a raging river on its way to the future.

AFTER ELAINE SENT HIM PACKING, Amador had plenty of time on his hands.

One afternoon he was lying on the living room floor in the basement apartment, notebook and pen lying by his head, when Pilar walked in. The sight of her son laid out on the old industrial carpet like a corpse made her gasp.

"What are you doing here, Ma?" Amador said as he rolled head and torso toward her.

What was *she* doing there?

She had been sent home early from the hospital laundry room because of an electrical fire. *She* had decided to put her free time to use by doing a little cleaning for her son. *She* wanted to know what he was doing lying on the floor like someone stabbed in the heart when he should be at work graphic designing.

Before he could put his mother on the spot by issuing as dubious a remark as *I'm not feeling too well today, Ma*, Pilar spared her only son the indignity by asking him a question she already knew the answer to, "So they fired you?"

Ramiro and Pilar had long before put two and two together regarding the nature of Amador's *Marketing Specialist* title, and he knew they rued the day they had kept silent while he tried to convince them it made more sense to choose *that* job over the apprenticeship at Nethercott's architecture firm in New York.

"So they fired you?" Pilar repeated.

"Ma, how can I be collecting unemployment then?" he said.

Pilar was willing to run with it and over dinner did her best to take pressure off her son by smiling as she announced to Ramiro and the girls, "Well, then, we have some news. Amador has been laid off."

Ramiro studied his son for a half minute. Then he turned his attention to his wife. He shook his head. He wasn't buying it, not for a second. Neither was Pilar, for that matter, but the couple had a history of engaging unpleasantness from different angles.

"He was fired, no? That's what you mean to say. He was fired."

Pilar put out her hand as if she were collecting raindrops and said, "But Ramiro, how can he be getting paid unemployment if he was fired?"

Ramiro, still stinging from his son's *no* to Nethercott just a few months ago, shook his head and repeated what he had said but with an inflection now tinged with sadness and cynicism.

"He was fired. That is what you meant to say, Pilar."

Pilar tilted her head, put out her hand to collect more raindrops, and pretended to ponder Ramiro's words for several seconds before responding.

"But Ramiro, how can that be if he is receiving money from unemployment?"

Ramiro sighed and shook his head. Sara and Elena, home from college and gaining daily in worldly sophistication, chimed in.

"My God, Pa, you can't just say things are true without having evidence," Elena said.

Sara agreed. "Pa, you've always talked about the Fascists in Spain, how *they* decided what was and wasn't true solely based on what they wanted people to believe was true, regardless of the facts. Isn't that what you're doing right now?"

Silence.

"Well, isn't it?"

"Sara," Pilar warned.

The chair fell back as Ramiro jumped to his feet and slammed his fist on the table.

"I AM YOUR FATHER!"

The words sprang forth like desperate hands, grabbing each of them by the chin and twisting each head toward Ramiro's own besieged face. He couldn't look at them for too long and glanced away, disgusted with himself more than with his children.

A shared heaviness, a sense of family failure and embarrassment weighed down upon the Santiagos. One by one they bowed their heads.

Amador stared at his father's plate and felt an overwhelming sense of the past careening into the present. He wanted to offer a word of encouragement on behalf of them all, make some gesture of atonement.

But what words? And what gestures? He had lost all credibility. Nothing for any of them to do but remain silent, ride out the next few minutes. No flying plate this time. The moment had passed. Five years had passed.

And what a sad strange episode that had been. The plate's brief flight had seemed to endow it with life, given it voice.

Surely, they were all remembering the plate. But did they remember what the plate had said? Did the twins understand how easy it was to forget the things that once mattered, the things that should still and always matter?

The conversation that day had begun innocently enough. The Broadway musical, *Man of La Mancha*, had finally closed. Pilar had gone in the fall to see it on a chartered bus filled with other *Club España* ladies.

What a wonderful time they had had. What splendid voices they had heard. Pilar told her family how on the ride back to Newark they had talked about the meaning of the *Impossible Dream* and given their opinions.

She said walking out of the theater she had felt sad, but in a happy way, because what she had seen and heard had seemed so much bigger than life, and it had filled her with hope.

Amador remembered glancing at his father as his mother was speaking. Ramiro had pursed his lips and exhaled, as if in need of relief or greater patience. Motivated by his mother's words, a glass of wine, and his father's old-world stubbornness—and sampling a foretaste of independence bolstered by the advent of freshman orientation just days away—Amador decided then and there to throw down the gauntlet.

As usual, the twins—still two years from college at the time—sided with their brother.

Amador tried to explain to his father, the unschooled, self-educated immigrant construction worker, why poetry mattered, why it was relevant now more than ever given the preponderance of materialism and shallow thinking in the world.

Ramiro looked at his son as if he were deranged. Hadn't all that schooling taught him one single useful thing?

"And this *Poetry*," Ramiro said, "does she put food in your mouth? Does she put a roof over your head?" He made the word *Poetry* sound like the name of a whore.

Undeterred, the *luminaries*—as Ramiro referred to the twins and Amador when they were at their most *clever*—jabbered on.

When he could stomach no more, he shouted, "Enough!"

But it was hardly enough for Amador, whose ears were warm and whose brain was waltzing. He retaliated with a soft stream of passive aggressive murmurings: "Of course, sure, Pa, no doubt, clearly, yes-yes, uh-huh, uh-huh, right, right..."

Ramiro gazed at his son with a chilling look of distraction until the boy shut his mouth. Ramiro then looked down at his plate, and for a good while they all sat at the kitchen table listening to the measured sounds of the twins' forks clicking against their plates.

No one ever asked Pilar why she chose to speak just then. Perhaps thinking the silence would do more harm than good, or that the moment was ripe for a breakthrough, Pilar said, "What are we without our dreams, Ramiro? What is left of us if all we think about is food in our stomachs and a roof over our heads?"

When it happened, the act itself seemed to develop in slow motion and for an instant struck Amador as amusing rather than alarming, a moment plucked from a sitcom and inserted live into the little kitchen for the viewing pleasure and entertainment of the Santiagos.

Ramiro lurched up from his seat grasping the dinner plate like a discus. He hesitated a second, perhaps his subconscious mind determining that the effect he was seeking was unlikely, given the contents of the meal and an inbred reluctance by Ramiro to cause excess damage to Pilar's kitchen. Cabbage, potato, boiled meat and chickpeas were never designed to produce loud, startling noises.

When the plate crashed against the wall, having whizzed by inches from Amador's head, it produced a dull plop-crack noise. Pieces of food-padded porcelain dropped to the linoleum floor with muted thuds and clinks. Bits landed apologetically atop the China cabinet that had come all the way from Spain after Abuelo and Abuela died.

Ramiro slammed the door on his way out. Pilar warned her children with a look, *Not a word!*

How well she knew her husband!

Within seconds he was back, standing in the open doorway, glaring at his wife and children.

"THIS! *This* is what happens!" he roared and thrust his fist at the befouled wall.

He pressed his lips together, closed his eyes and shook his head. His voice became soft and unsettling. "To honor your father means nothing to you? Is God a fool to ask this of you? So help me, if I return to find that any one of you has tried to clean up this, this *mierda...*"

Ramiro looked at his wife and lifted his forefinger in the air, issuing a silent parting warning to all. Then he walked out the door and disappeared for hours.

There was always that aspect of the dramatic to Ramiro that perfectly complemented his stage actor voice, but even at his most aggrieved and self-righteous, he could never disown his generous heart.

Around midnight Amador woke with a full bladder and got up to go to the bathroom. It was the only bathroom, a tiny compartment attached to the kitchen.

Pilar was leaning in the small archway between the kitchen and the living room speaking to her husband. Ramiro was on his knees facing the far wall, wiping up the mess with a damp rag. A plastic bucket and a double brown bag sat on the floor next to him.

Amador stood behind his mother. Sensing her child's anxiety, Pilar turned, smiled and nodded, "Go on, there's no one in the bathroom."

He walked stiffly past his father. All he could think to say was "Hey, Pa." Ramiro ignored him.

Five years later there they were again. But a young man could change a lot in five years. He could develop a better feel for the baffling texture of love. He watched his father move stiffly away from the table. The aching man, aching of body, soul and heart.

I am your father.

Ramiro walked out of the kitchen. He turned on the television in the living room and sat on the couch to watch the evening news. Amador could hear that something important was happening out there in the world. Something important was always happening, and always about to happen.

But *the real world* was so much bigger than *that* world.

Listening to the fast easy reports emitting from the console television set, it struck Amador that a failure of words was not always a failure of truth.

Ramiro was not the most articulate man, nor was he right about everything. But he was right that he *was* and would always be his insufferable children's father. And that he, Amador, had indeed been fired, just as Ramiro had said.

AMADOR TELLS MAGGIE not to harbor bitterness in her heart because of compulsive corporate greed, widespread deception and hypocrisy, loss of home, etcetera, etcetera.

"Life does not forgive bitterness," he says.

"I'm not bitter," she says, "not usually."

She often thinks of Ramiro. God alone knows what kinds of things were going on in that poor man's head all those years living in America: the brutalities of the Spanish Civil War, the murdered father of ten tossed into a ditch, the lost childhood and wrecked dreams, the challenge of articulating a displaced life.

A different time and place, of course, and a different man. But she worries about Amador, who lugs around the burden of love and memory like a stoic.

What Amador needs is a good old-fashioned catharsis.

"Write as a means of catharsis," she tells him.

She probably worries too much. For the most part, Amador is philosophical about life. He jokes about their predicament, tells her he's thinking about driving to the old button factory in Newark to see if Mr. Nadelman will give him back his old job. He wonders if Elaine is still *presenting rearward*. He says working in the darkroom was the best job he ever had.

"You're right, Mags," he says. "I *should* write. I do have more time now."

But she is skeptical.

One day he tells Maggie he is setting aside his novel (that first draft of that first chapter about that recluse who suspects he is turning into a ghost).

Instead, he has begun working on a book that explores the connection between flamenco and jazz, doing lots of research and filling page after page with notes. Maggie remembers Amador telling her about a writer who spent four years researching and taking notes for an historical novel only to die halfway through a first draft of Chapter 1.

Amador considers it a labor of love. That's because Leo died and never got to write that book. It happened after the *Fiestas de San Fermín* in Pamplona, just a few months after Leo hugged Amador and put a thousand dollar check in his shirt pocket.

Death is bad enough, but hell, dying in a stupid car accident? Knowing Leo, given the choice, he would have preferred being gored to death while running with the bulls, no doubt about it.

Over tapas and drinks Carl Thackeray remarks, "If I had it to do over again, I wouldn't change a thing."

This happens in front of an enormous HDTV with the volume set to Low during a Super Bowl party.

For the most part, the game serves as a screensaver. Everyone is drinking and in an elevated metaphysical state. Everyone is talking about life.

"What did you say, Carl?" Amador says.

Amador knows what Carl said, but he wants everyone to listen. Everyone stops to listen.

"I said, if I had it to do over again, I wouldn't change a thing."

"I thought you did, I thought you said that," Amador says. "Do you really believe that, Carl?"

"Uh, yeah? I'm happy to say I do," Carl says with a questioning smile.

"You should not be happy about that, Carl."

Factoring in the heavy drinking, the celebratory occasion, the heightened metaphysical state of all the souls gathered before the gigantic television screen, Amador's words still manage to surprise.

No one knows what to say.

Carl is an accountant, does the Santiago tax returns. A regular guy, maybe a little inclined toward vanity and self-complacency, a bit of a flirt sometimes, according to Maggie, who knows firsthand. Amador shakes his head ambiguously. Is he regretting what he said or what Carl said?

"Carl, that kind of thinking is what's wrong with the world. It suggests that every single decision you made in your life was the right one. Let's not kid ourselves. Only one person in history has known perfection. The rest of us are either trying to get it right or we're not, and if we're not, then hell, what's the point?"

Carl frowns for a moment, as if he is considering a counter-argument, but then he says, "Hey, what did we just miss?"

Someone turns up the volume. A wide receiver is dancing a polka with himself in the endzone while deferential teammates watch and wait for him to finish so they can celebrate.

The game has reasserted itself. People want to know what the score is, want to compare quarterback stats, want to know who the lineman limping off the field is. What's his name?

Later, though, Maggie overhears a few folks talking about what Amador said.

ONE DAY AMADOR gets home from his part-time job in Lumber (at Home Depot) and says, "If I had accepted that apprenticeship in New York, we wouldn't be in this fix."

Maggie gives him a look that's mostly compassion but with a dash of irony.

"Amador, listen to me. You can't go there."

"Why can't I?"

"What happened to being philosophical? Look, the important stuff isn't going to change. But you *will* have less space to putter."

"I can putter in the garage. We have to have a garage."

"We're still going to be who we are."

"Go on."

"And besides, there's a reason things happen the way they do. Don't you believe that?"

He thinks about it.

"I don't know, Mags, things happen to people, good things and bad things. You either face up to them or you run and hide."

"What you just said. Fight or flight. Everything that happens to you forces you to respond in some way, right? You have to make a decision. So you add up all those decisions to get who you are, and then you take a look at who you are and maybe you ask yourself, is this it? Am I satisfied? Or is there more of me that needs or wants to be? And there's always more, isn't there? So maybe there is a reason for everything that happens. What do you think?"

"I see what you did there, Maggie. Brilliant. I do have to say, brilliant."

After dinner Amador says, "This is how I remember Ramiro and Pilar."

He stares at his wife, the mother of his children, the grandmother of his grandchildren. This is not the first time, so she knows how it will go.

Amador gets up, walks to the bay window and stares at the trees in the front yard for a minute or so. He comes back and speaks to her in a steady voice.

"I see her at midnight standing in the doorway between the living room and the kitchen back in Newark. She is speaking to him, her voice soothing his wounded pride and exonerating him of any wrongdoing. He's on his knees, his back to us, his head bowed, and he's cleaning up the mess, the one we all made together...

"Leo would have been all over it, Maggie. It's like I'm back in the darkroom at the button factory, working in that psychoactive red light, thinking about life, agitating negatives in the developer tray and bringing photo images to life, fixing them at the perfect moment, the way Leo showed me, negatives turned into positives and saved for posterity. I can almost feel him leaning over my shoulder, Maggie. He's all excited, pointing at Pa, reminding me what matters most:

That's what I'm talking about, Amador! Fix it right there, my man, and don't ever forget what's real."

About the Author

R. Garcia Vazquez was in grade school when he showed a classmate an episode he had scribbled for the popular TV series of the 1960's, "The Man from U.N.C.L.E." His writing passion persisted throughout decades, through countless ideas and drafts, and an eclectic series of jobs, including photography darkroom manager, security systems technician, college writing instructor, desktop publisher, newsletter editor, and technical writer. Work and raising a family kept him busy. At age 63, a year after retiring, he published his first novel, proving to himself and others that you are never too old to pursue your passion.

Garcia Vazquez's fiction incorporates psychological, spiritual, and surreal elements, and has been described by professional and lay reviewers as masterful, original, unpredictable, and haunting. He was born and raised in the melting pot Ironbound section of Newark, New Jersey (USA), the son of Galician Spaniards who taught him how to be human.

If you enjoyed *No Other Pearl*, please take a minute to leave a review on Amazon. Thank you!

Also by the author, and available on Amazon:

Mr. Galaxy's Unfinished Dream, a novel
Beneath An Alien Sun, a post-apocalyptic novel
The God of Beautiful Sorrows, a short story

For more information:
rgarciavazquez.com, facebook.com/rgvtimeleaper/

www.ingramcontent.com/pod-product-compliance
Lightning Source LLC
Chambersburg PA
CBHW020407150626
46554CB00012B/412